ABOUT ....

James Warden was a teacher for forty years and retired in 2006. He now enjoys his retirement as much as he enjoyed his time in the education service and is catching up on those things which he left undone and ought to have done – in particular, his writing. He writes every morning between nine o'clock and noon, for thirty-six weeks of the year.

He is fortunate enough to be able to act in several Norwich theatres – the Maddermarket, the Sewell Barn and, with the Great Hall Players, at the Assembly House – and this experience informs his writing. His stage adaptation of Laurie Lee's *As I Walked Out One Midsummer Morning* was performed at the Sewell Barn Theatre in November 2009. His original play, *Letters from a Boy in the Trenches*, which was based on the letters of a WW1 soldier, was performed in Marchington, Staffordshire in 2015.

James is married – for the second time – and lives in Norfolk. He and his wife travel as much as possible. They have visited Italy (where they were married in 2002) several times, Canada, Bermuda, Egypt, India, the Czech Republic, New England, Poland, Slovenia, Antarctica, the Falkland Islands, Alaska, the Galapagos Islands, Australia and Switzerland. In 2018, they travelled across the USA on Route 66. They have also taken several holidays in various Mediterranean resorts

– the basis for his first novel, *Three Women of a Certain Age*, which was published in July 2010.

During his years in education, he wrote about twenty play scripts for children. These included the one that formed the basis for his children's story, *The Great Gobbler and his Home Baking Factory at the North Pole*, which he wrote in 1982 and published in December 2010.

He has three sons by his first marriage, and they inspired three of his novels – *The Vampire's Homecoming*, published in 2011, *The One-eyed Dwarf*, published in 2012 and *The Haunting of Thornham Staithe*, published in 2022. With them and his first wife, he also travelled to the southern states of North America, France, Germany (West and East), Estonia and what was Czechoslovakia.

WRITING BY JAMES WARDEN

<u>Stories of Our Time</u>
Three Women of a Certain Age (2010)
The Age of Wisdom (2015))
Swinging in the Sixties (2016)

<u>'Tales of Mystery and Imagination'</u>
The Vampire's Homecoming (2011)
The First Rendlesham Incident (2017)
The Search for Edwin Drood (2020)
The Haunting of Thornham Staithe (2022)

<u>Stories for Children</u>
The Great Gobbler and his Home-Baking Factory at
the North Pole (2010)
The One-eyed Dwarf (2012)

<u>Biography</u>
The Boy in the Photograph: Bill Pieri's
autobiography (2014)
A Child of the Fifties: autobiography of my
childhood (2017)

<u>Plays</u>
As I Walked Out One Midsummer Morning
*(Adapted with the permission of Laurie Lee's estate
and performed at the Sewell Barn Theatre in
Norwich in November 2009.)*

Letters from a Boy in the Trenches
*(Adapted from the letters home of Sydney Harrison
and performed by the Marchington Amateur Dramatic
Society in November 2015.)*

BINGHAM AND THE TRAVELLER'S DAUGHTER

BY

JAMES WARDEN

Grosvenor House
Publishing Limited

The book cover is copyright to James Warden

This book is published by
Grosvenor House Publishing Ltd
Link House
140 The Broadway, Tolworth, Surrey, KT6 7HT.
www.grosvenorhousepublishing.co.uk

This book is a work of fiction. Any resemblance to
people or events, past or present, is purely coincidental.

A CIP record for this book
is available from the British Library

ISBN: 978-1-80381-175-8

Chapter One
A SCOWL ON HIS FACE

The flautist had been playing for some time before the travellers arrived in their lorry. He had taken his stand near the door of the public house and the cap he'd positioned on the pavement was already showing signs of the customers' appreciation. The Cairn terrier on the rug beside him looked up at the man, catching his glance occasionally and seeming to wonder; it was clear to even a casual observer that they knew and trusted each other.

This wasn't lost on the traveller who led the others from his lorry – he knew animals as well as he knew people (perhaps better) – and neither were the clothes the musician was wearing: a long, riding coat that had seen better days but was from a well-known tailoring firm, a matching fedora of similar age, a pair of chinos and an open-necked chambray shirt that placed the player in his seventies. Here was someone down on his luck.

The leader of the travellers, a scowl on his face, unrolled a fold of banknotes and dropped a tenner into the cap. The flautist nodded his appreciation without interrupting the smooth rhythm of the song he was playing, a song the man knew but could not identify.

It was a warm night in late May; spring had conjured an early summer and people were enjoying the sunshine and a warm breeze from the south. The travellers had been working hard all day and were eager to start drinking; but for their thirst, the flautist knew that the scowling man would have enquired as to the name of the tune.

The pub, The Albion, was situated partway between the town and the common and attracted locals from nearby villages as well as townspeople and passers-by out for an evening drive. It was a welcoming establishment and the landlord had provided a bowl of clean water for the terrier and brought a pint for the flautist soon after he started playing; another arrived once the travellers had placed their orders.

Neat, privet hedges screened the carpark from the seating area, where people gathered as the evening wore on. The flautist continued playing a selection of Irish folk songs and sentimental popular tunes before finding a seat for himself to drink his pint. He chose one away from the customers in a quiet corner, placing the rucksack that contained his belongings on the seat beside him. The terrier sat further along the bench, watching and waiting for the titbit he knew would appear in the man's hand.

None of the other customers seemed to object to his presence any more than they did to that of the travellers when they decided to sit outside. The men were smartly dressed in designer jeans and check shirts, their skin shining, and their hair sleeked down or twisted into quiffs and waves.

"What was that song you were playing when we arrived?" asked their leader.

The flautist looked up and smiled.

"It was one my grandmother used to hum to my younger sister," he replied in an unmistakeable Dublin accent, "It's the melody line to *Crowley's Reel*."

"You from the home country?"

"God's own country," replied the flautist.

The questioner returned to his drinking. Fresh glasses of beer appeared and soon the table was cluttered with empties. The travellers continued to talk among themselves: their voices loud and beery, their laughter raucous. In the warmth of that evening, no one objected. Whenever another group of locals arrived and found a free table, the sound of their voices was also carried on the softly moving air and wafted away beyond the railway line and the motorway from where, occasionally, the passing of trains and cars could be heard.

After half-an-hour or so, the flautist resumed his playing and this time he chose songs they all knew but whose names they could not quite remember: *El Condor Pasa, La Vie En Rose, Smoke Gets in Your Eyes, The Windmills of Your Mind*. It annoyed them as they listened, and yet the tunes stirred memories they could not forget.

Eventually, the leader of the travellers, his scowl deepened with drink, stumbled over to the flautist.

"You're a Dublin man, are you not?" he asked, his voice a slur.

"Sandycove," replied the musician.

"Ah, one of the posh people then?"

"It was a while ago. I've lived over here a long time."

The mind of the traveller's leader was clearly muddled, and not only by drink: several thoughts, perhaps needs, were racing through it at one and the same instant.

"You've come upon hard times?"

"There's no fool like an old fool," replied the flautist.

"Women trouble, is it?"

"I married a young one with children – a woman I met in Bulgaria and brought over here for a better life. When love flew out of the window, I lost my home. The court ruled that the children needed it more than I did ... It didn't help when I lost my job."

"I might be able to put something your way. Are you any good with your hands?"

"I can lay a driveway, run up a fence or two and put a shed together."

"Then you could be the man for me. Twenty-five a day, your meals provided, and no questions asked."

"I could earn that playing on the street."

"On a good day, maybe, but not when the weather turns. I'm talking every day. Let's say forty quid and meals. That's my last offer."

"Done," replied the flautist, extending his hand.

"Amos O'Leary," said the traveller, spitting on his hand and taking the flautist's. "Your hands aren't the hands of a workman,"

"It's been a while. They'll harden off. The name's Joyce – Michael Joyce."

A smile crossed Amos O'Leary's face, a smile that was still there when he and his friends drove off just after dark closed in on the drinkers. The travellers were crowded into the cab of the old lorry, while the flautist sat in the open back, glad his rucksack softened the trip over country lanes, cradling his dog and cooing its name occasionally.

And so, it was that Bingham came to the travellers' camp near Chertsey.

*

Three days before, he had been sitting in his kitchen at Bob's Farm enjoying a cup of black coffee and one of Lina's welcome scones, dripping with jam and cream, when Ben, the Cairn terrier, uttered his sharp, raucous, little bark and rushed to the stable door. Bingham had heard nothing.

A man leaned on the lower part of the door, reaching over and into the kitchen. He was what the comics Bingham had enjoyed as a boy in Wolverhampton described as 'a mountain of a man' and he filled the doorway.

"Mr Bingham, are you?"

"That's right," replied Bingham without moving from the table, continuing in his softest voice, "Ben, come over here."

The terrier responded but not without looking over his shoulder several times in the direction of the door and delivering a few more warning barks of discontentment.

"I'm Patrick Dolan, known as Paddy," continued the man who Bingham decided was a traveller of some kind.

He was an old man, probably near to Bingham in age, but time did not seem to have withered his strength or his toughness. His muscles might have been old, but they looked rock solid and the back of his hands were covered in callouses. He made no attempt to enter the kitchen until Bingham invited him to do so.

"Would you like a coffee and one of my wife's scones?"

"I'd prefer a mug of tea if it's no trouble, as strong as you can brew it."

The tea delivered and Bingham's black coffee replenished, the two men viewed each other across the orderly array of Lina's table; walnut oil, Dijon mustard, a variety of salad leaves and a handful of black olives sat alongside a thin baguette and a packet of goat's cheese.

"My wife is in the vegetable garden," said Bingham with his usual cheery smile, "hoping for a few sprigs of broccoli."

"I'm looking for you to help me find my granddaughter, Mr Bingham."

"You're a travelling man, aren't you, Paddy? Why come to me? I thought you people kept yourselves to yourselves. Is there no one among you who can find your granddaughter?"

"You're a man who comes straight to the point, Mr Bingham."

"You don't waste too much time yourself, Paddy. But before you begin, tell me how you came to find me out here in the wilds of Suffolk."

"My wife and I live at Martlesham. She reads a lot – I've never learned myself – and she remembers you and the little girl."

"Your trailer is at Martlesham?"

"No. Mary and I live in a bungalow now, but we're still travellers, you see. Once a traveller, always a traveller. I'm willing to pay. Money's never been a problem with us. How much will I be owing you on account?"

As he spoke, Paddy Dolan took from his pocket a thick wad of bank notes and began counting them onto the table.

"Tell me about your granddaughter first, Paddy. We can discuss terms later," said Bingham, eager to slow matters down.

What he knew about travellers was mainly through hearsay, but his own experiences with them had not been good. While he was teaching at a Midlands' school in 1970, a group of them had set up camp on a nearby common and left it in a filthy state: paper and soiled packets, food waste and excreta everywhere, old mattresses slung into trees, rusty gas cylinders discarded, dirty clothes left in piles, tins and bottles dumped, the earth scorched. After the police had evicted the group, the common – normally a playground for the school children – had been unusable for months; later, the council had sealed off the land from the road with a dry moat and mounds and erected a low, iron archway to prevent any vehicle other than cars from entering.

Yet the man sitting opposite him across the kitchen table was as clean as a whistle, shining with health, smartly dressed, his shirt sleeves and trousers showing the signs of having been ironed.

"My granddaughter, Lizzie, would phone me every week, sometimes oftener. I love her, you know, and she loves me. Every weekend she'd phone without fail, every Sunday always, come hell or high water. A week ago, now, she never phoned. I was worried. I phoned her mammy, but got no sense out of her ..."

"Her mother would be your daughter rather than your daughter-in-law?"

"That's right – her mammy. I went to see her, but still got nothing. My son-in-law stayed out of my way. We've never got on."

"What did your daughter say?"

"She said that Lizzie – her name's Elizabeth but everyone knows her as Lizzie – had just gone off. She took nothing with her, not a toothbrush even, nothing – no money, nothing. She went in the night when the camp was asleep. No one in the camp was any help, either – no one knew a thing or wouldn't say.

"I wandered about hoping to find someone who might have seen her. They were in the Midlands at the time. I wandered down to the canal and along the towpath."

"Had her parents searched for her?"

"Martha said they had but I'm not sure she was being completely honest with me."

"Why wouldn't she be?"

"I'm not sure ... she ... Let me finish. There were some bargees moored along the towpath. They thought they might have heard voices in the early hours of the morning going towards the next village. So, I went there. People aren't fond of us travellers, as you may know, and at first I got nothing but backs turned on me, but then someone told me that a car had been stolen the night Lizzie left and that gyppos were to blame."

"How did they know that?"

"They didn't, but we're the usual scapegoats."

"But you believed them?"

"I did wonder."

"You think your granddaughter would have stolen a car? How old was she? Could she drive?"

"A goodly number of us drive, Mr Bingham, it's a way of life – but, no, I didn't think Lizzie would have stolen a car ..."

"You think she wasn't alone?"

"That's right. I don't know anything else, but the car was found the next day in London. I think Lizzie may have gone there."

"Is this why you've come to me rather than asking among your own people?"

"I want her found, Mr Bingham, and brought back."

"You enquired no further?

"No."

"How old is your granddaughter?"

"I'm not sure. We don't celebrate birthdays. She'd be about fifteen or so."

"Has she any relatives in London?"

"She's not with them."

"So, you did enquire further?"

"Not too much further."

"Is there nothing else you can tell me?"

"No, but I'm able to pay."

It was obvious to Bingham that Paddy Dolan suspected more than he was prepared to confide; whether he knew more, Bingham was unsure. The man seemed honest enough but was clearly someone who came from a group of people who kept themselves to themselves, a quality that was of little use when searching for a missing person.

He had no stomach for what would prove to be a difficult task and in emotional terms probably an unrewarding one: successful or not, he would end up with little or no thanks.

"My terms are £200 a day plus expenses," he said.

"Will a week on account be all right, and we'll settle when you've found Lizzie?" replied the travelling man, unrolling fourteen hundred pounds onto the table.

The last time Bingham had seen that amount of money at a glance was when his bees had worked all year to provide it, and he couldn't help wondering how Paddy Dolan could be so ready to hand it out without a flinch, as though it was merely pocket money.

"A photograph of your granddaughter would be useful, Mr Dolan, and I'll need your phone number in case I find her."

"How do you propose to go about doing just that, Mr Bingham?"

"I don't know. I shall need to enquire among your people and from what you say they'll not speak to me."

"Have you heard of a dossa?"

"You mean homeless people?"

"And derelicts. If they're useful with their hands, we sometimes take them on. There's always work to do, and a good workman is always useful. We're never idle and I happen to know that my son-in-law has a lot of work going at this time. His name's Amos – Amos O'Leary – and you'll find him on a site at Chertsey."

"I thought you said they were in the Midlands?"

"They moved – they were planning to move, anyway – as soon as Lizzie left."

Bingham smiled to himself as he slipped the money into his shirt pocket. What Lina would say he wasn't sure, but Paddy Dolan's suggestion fleshed itself out in his mind as soon as the traveller spoke, and it was years since he'd played the flute, a skill he'd acquired while still at school.

*

The lorry rattled to a halt beside a row of trailers. Within seconds, the travellers had piled out and disappeared into their respective homes. Amos O'Leary approached Bingham, with a smile on his face. It wasn't a pleasant one.

"You'll not mind spending the night in the back of the lorry, will you, Joyce? I'll send the missus out with a blanket."

Bingham wondered what he'd let himself in for as he struggled from the lorry and turned to help Ben to the ground. He was still wondering, when a fat woman, made up to the nines and wearing a blush pink nightdress, emerged from O'Leary's trailer and handed him two heavy blankets.

"Martha O'Leary," she said with a smile, "I'm pleased to meet you. It may get chilly in the early hours. You might need a couple of blankets. Has the little dog been fed?"

"Yes, thank you. He always has his evening meal at four o'clock."

Martha O'Leary laughed, and both she and Bingham knew why: the man's manner of speech and the dog's routine were a novelty.

"He seems a perky, little chap," she said, kneeling to fondle the terrier's ears, "You'd best be careful. There're some funny buggers on the site could take a fancy to a dog like him."

She looked up at Bingham

"Are you sure you're up to the work? He'll drive you hard, and you're no spring chicken. Come on hard times, have you?"

"A domestic: I've lost my home."

"I'm sorry to hear that. I don't know what I'd do if I hadn't a place of me own."

She bade Bingham goodnight and went back to her bedroom, while Bingham picked up his rucksack and made for what appeared to be a toilet block. It might have served that purpose at one time, but he failed to find an unbroken shower head, a sink that wasn't chipped or a window that wasn't smashed. Most of the toilets were blocked and some were overflowing with waste and soiled paper. He supposed the O'Learys had washing facilities in their trailer, but judged he wasn't to be allowed beyond the doorstep as he looked for a clean basin over which to brush his teeth.

Chapter Two

WITHOUT THE TRACE OF AN ACCENT

Bingham was woken the next morning, soon after the sun rose, by a little girl holding a plate piled with what the restaurants describe as a Full English Breakfast.

"Me mam says here's your breakfast and me da says you'd better be ready to go in half-an-hour."

"What's your name?"

The girl, who must have been six or seven, was still in her nightclothes. She looked Bingham up and down, the expression on her face suggesting she was considering whether it was worth her while to grace him with an answer.

"Mary."

"Have you any brothers or sisters?"

"Me da says be ready in half-an-hour," replied the girl, turning on her heels and making for the caravan with a flounce in her walk.

Bingham gazed at the breakfast and realized it would take him at least that amount of time to eat it even if eating it was an option. Given that his normal portion was an egg or something similar on one round of toast and that he hadn't eaten meat since coming across a slaughterhouse in Wolverhampton when he was a young man, it wasn't. He glanced at Ben who was eyeing the bacon and sausages.

"Are you going to help me out, my son – hmm? I don't suppose it will hurt you just for once, will it, but don't tell Lina."

While the Cairn polished off the meat, Bingham waded through the eggs, toast, beans, mushrooms, tomatoes and hash browns. The breakfast was well-cooked in an old-fashioned way, and eating it reminded him of weekends spent with his grandmother. As a boy, he'd enjoyed her breakfasts, well-laced with fat, but his stomach was older now and having struggled with one of the hash browns he gave the other to Ben "as a treat".

He'd never gone to work in his life without washing himself after a night's sleep but saw that neither time nor facilities favoured him. He walked Ben across to the toilet block where they both did what they felt necessary, although it distressed Bingham to break the habit of years, yet again, when he found nowhere to dispose of his dog's waste.

"Are you right then? We haven't got all day!"

O'Leary's voice belted out across the campsite and other travellers, also busy preparing their lorries for the day's work, looked up.

"You've a dossa, then, Amos?" cried one, "Don't you work the old man too hard."

"He can leave the terrier here. It'll be in the way, tarmacking."

"You hear that, Joyce? The dog stays."

Bingham said nothing in reply to either man. He suddenly felt threatened and his reaction was to take refuge in taciturnity: he'd often found when dealing with bullies that silence said more than words.

"He can't go in those clothes, Amos. The tar'll ruin them," cried Martha from the door of her trailer.

"I'm not waiting," replied her husband, who was dressed smartly in an immaculate three-piece pinstriped suit and patent leather shoes.

"Here, just a minute."

O'Leary's wife, obstinate as her husband, disappeared for a moment to return with a pair of dark blue overalls, spotlessly clean with pin-sharp creases.

"Put these on, Mr Joyce. They'll keep the tar off of your clothes. I'll look after the little dog if you like. He'll come to no harm with me."

"Thanks, Mrs O'Leary, but it's all right. He's a rescue and he's used to me and my ways."

She looked Bingham up and down in the same way her daughter had done, as though distrusting his explanation, thought the better of it, gave him a quick smile and stood watching until the lorry had disappeared along the track.

The back of the lorry having been loaded with tar drums Bingham was told to get into the cab where he pulled on the boiler suit.

"Driveways are my speciality. You'll soon pick up the hang of things."

Amos O'Leary said no more, as he drove hell for leather along country roads until they came to a quarry where piles of pink grit were waiting.

"Take the shovel and get busy."

O'Leary nodded towards the back of the lorry where a selection of tools, wrapped neatly in sacking, was stowed beneath the tar drums.

As he bent to his task, Bingham wondered who had loaded the drums, since O'Leary's own boiler suit, which was hung neatly in the cab beside him, showed no signs of work. He supposed the job must have been done while he was washing his face, and whoever did it must have worked at speed and been of prodigious strength because the drums looked heavy. Not for the first time that morning, Bingham felt threatened.

He supposed the grit to be the waste left over once conventional builders had taken their loads because it was seventy percent dust. Bingham was both relieved and troubled: relieved that each shovelful was lighter than he'd expected, troubled as to what plans O'Leary had for the grit's use.

When the lorry was loaded, Bingham thanked Martha quietly for the boiler suit: it was covered in pink dust and his clothes, the only ones he had, would have been unwearable at the end of the day. O'Leary smiled as he looked Bingham up and down. Bingham could see in the man's eyes that it was a smile tempered with regret.

As they made their way into town, Doris Day sang a selection of her songs: *When I Fall in Love, Bewitched Bothered and Bewildered, Secret Love, Move over Darling, Sentimental Journey*. Amos knew all the words and joined in with a voice that was melodic and chaotic. When they came to *Sentimental Journey*, Bingham laughed.

"What's so funny?"

"It was one of my mother's favourites," Bingham lied, feeling that O'Leary might miss the irony of the song's title with regard to their present trip.

"I'm very fond of Doris Day ... and Roy Orbison ... that kind of music. I like it. Now, to business. Come to think of it, the dog might be handy. They like dogs, and trust people with them."

"They?"

"The pensioners. We're headed for Pensioners Row," laughed O'Leary, "I can smell a pensioner a mile off. Keep your eyes open for driveways."

The hunt was on and O'Leary was like a man possessed. As a boy, Bingham had been taught to use a shotgun by his maternal grandfather who owned a Beagle. The animal would sniff the air relentlessly and as soon as prey was scented the dog froze and stared fixedly in its direction. O'Leary reminded Bingham of that dog.

The lorry wove its way through the outskirts of Chertsey until O'Leary was satisfied he'd found his quarry. He pulled the vehicle to a gentle stop beside the curb of a likely house and looked at himself in the rear-view mirror.

"Stay where you are. I don't want them to see you covered in dust. But let the little fella look out of the window. If he doesn't bark, give him a poke. I want them to notice his face. That dog's face could be worth a fortune."

O'Leary checked his suit, was satisfied it looked immaculate, dropped neatly from the cab, made his way through the little gate and rang a ship's bell that hung by the side of the door. There was a rattle of keys and some scraping of the lock but eventually the door was opened.

A blonde woman, her hair tousled, smiled at O'Leary. She was still in her bathrobe, her face fresh from the shower.

"I'm sorry to disturb you, madam, but I think if you see what I have to offer you'll not be objecting to my presence on your doorstep."

Bingham smiled to himself, realizing that Amos O'Leary spoke without the trace of an accent. There was still a hint of his roots in the phrasing and the Irish charm was unmistakeable but the voice was what used to be called BBC English.

"I am in rather a hurry," replied the woman, pointing at her hair.

"A moment of your time, madam, could prove to be a turning point in your life."

Bingham observed that O'Leary paused to smile but not long enough for the woman to interrupt. While he spoke, the traveller's eyes never left her face.

"I happen to be in the area, working on a job just round the corner from here, and as we passed your driveway I noticed that it was breaking up in places. As it happens, we over-estimated the amount of tar we'd need for the other work, and rather than let it go to waste I thought we could do both of us a favour. I could make good use of the tar and my time, and you could have a brand-new driveway – all for the ridiculously low price of twenty-five pounds."

"My husband is at work. I would need …"

"Don't let me press you, madam, but think of his face when he arrives home tonight to find his driveway as good as new and a weight off his mind if he was thinking of having to get it done at the regular price, as I'm sure he was. Make his day, madam. Offers like this don't come to us very often. I know this area well. We were involved with the original builders. We may even have laid your driveway."

Bingham couldn't help himself: he smiled. His respect for an artist of any kind went without saying. Once, he'd even admired a conman – an antique dealer selling a reproduction of an eighteenth-century mahogany side table as an original to someone with more money than sense. Bingham would have been taken in completely; it was only the knowledge of his daughter, Cecilia, who was hunting for period furniture herself at the time, that made Bingham realise the antique dealer was a fraudster. Watching O'Leary at work, now, brought back the memory. The man was an artist.

Bingham looked at the woman's face. She was an attractive person in her sixties – nobody's fool under most circumstances but susceptible to charm. What did Laurie Lee have to say about charm in his essay on the subject? 'Charm is the ultimate weapon, the supreme seduction, against which there are few defences.' The old charmer was right. Bingham could see the woman being taken in by O'Leary; he could see the excitement in her face as she pictured her husband arriving home. The offer was too much to resist. Life is for living. Seize the moment. The tired old phrases appeared in her eyes and her smiles.

"Twenty-five pounds you say?"

"Twenty-five pounds and not a penny more."

"Very well. I think my husband will be pleased."

"Madam, I can see his face now."

O'Leary bowed slightly as the woman closed her front door, hurrying in to find the money and get dressed. His face, as he turned back to the lorry, was alive with delight. He nodded Bingham out of the cab and set him to work clearing the weeds.

Although he knew he was being drawn into the fraudulent scheme, Bingham felt he could do nothing about his predicament: to protest would be to jeopardise his purpose. He looked at Ben, who sat watching, pursed his lips and shrugged his shoulders; even the dog seemed to understand that he was complicit in the deception.

Sitting on the back of the lorry, his legs dangling, O'Leary watched Bingham, impatience apparent in every line of his body. He looked about him as though he thought the husband might return at any moment or a bobby on the beat might stroll round the corner. Bingham thought there was a fat chance of that happening.

"Hurry up, man, there's no need to clear every bloody weed, just the ones that might stick up through the grit."

Bingham ignored the comment. Observing the state of the driveway, he saw that not only had the original surfacing split but that it had been laid on sand, which was now working its way up through the tarmac; the lumps and bumps were due to subsidence.

"There's no point in pouring more tarmac and grit over this mess," he said, "It needs to be dug out completely and a hard-core base put down."

"When I want your opinion, I'll ask for it. Who do you think you are – the fecking planning inspector? Get over here and give me a fecking hand with this tar barrel."

Bingham only hesitated for a moment, realizing he had no choice. As they spread the tar, he also realized that it was watered-down, thin as mud, and mud was what it would be after a good shower of rain, sticky mud running out onto the road, a mess and nothing more.

It was no more than fifteen minutes work to cover the driveway, and then O'Leary said to Bingham:

"Get spreading the grit – and go easy on the shovelfuls. We can get a few more in today."

As Bingham worked, he heard O'Leary at the front door. His deafness amidst the rattling of the grit on the shovel made it difficult to hear exactly what was said but the drift was clear and he could read the woman's lips as she said:

"Two hundred and fifty pounds?"

O'Leary had meant twenty-five pounds a square yard. The crafty bugger thought Bingham.

"But I don't have that kind of money in the house," cried the woman, her voice shrill and tearful.

"That's no problem, madam. There's a cash machine down the road by the supermarket. Hop in the lorry and I'll run you down myself."

Always, O'Leary appeared to be doing his customer a favour: the mistake was hers, but he'd get her out of the mess she was in. After all, two hundred and fifty pounds for ten square yards of driveway was a gift, and "who can look a gift horse in the mouth?"

Bingham heard the last remark as the lorry pulled away from the curb. He completed the spreading of the grit and laid the shovel in the wheelbarrow. It was going to be a long day, and he was tired already. Bingham was unused to heavy, physical work unless it was occasionally and at his own pace. The muscle in his back, which he'd pulled out of place arranging chairs for a parents' meeting at his school some years before, was playing up again and would be severely upset by the time evening arrived. His hands were dry and the skin had come away in places. His old, slack muscles felt wrenched out of place; the pain in his knees told him it was time for a coffee break. Poor old sod, he thought, laughing to himself and thinking of his mother's generation and their stoicism born of war.

His pain was to be repeated over and over again that day, and O'Leary made no attempt to help him unless speed was essential: Bingham found himself spreading the tar as well as the grit while the traveller scouted round for more customers.

They resurfaced nine driveways and were clear of the area and rolling home, this time accompanied by Roy Orbison, by late afternoon. Lunch had been a few pasties and some custard tarts, picked up at a local baker's shop, washed down with cans of fizzy drink. Bingham felt sick at heart as well as in his stomach, but Amos O'Leary was cock-a-hoop: Bingham estimated the roll of banknotes in the man's pocket must amount to the best part of two thousand pounds, which wasn't bad for a day's work.

The bounce in the man's step as he leapt from the lorry and made his way to the family trailer said it all as far as his satisfaction was concerned.

"Just a moment," said Bingham.

"What's up, Joyce?"

"You owe me forty pounds, I believe."

The hesitation was significant and the anger apparent in the traveller's look.

"You finish up, first. There's those tar barrels to see to."

They'd stopped off on the way back to pick up a fresh tar barrel from a roadworks store. Bingham had watched the transaction and noticed both men involved watching him, but it wasn't until now that he appreciated what his part in the transaction was to be.

"You water them down, ejit. We'll get another three barrels from the one I bought."

It was hard work and would have been even if Bingham wasn't already exhausted. Anger and stubbornness kept him going: the first because of his predicament, the second inherited from his mother. He'd spent a day with these people and learned nothing. If every day was to follow the same pattern, he'd have no time for the questions he needed to ask. It was six o'clock before he'd completed the task and seven before he'd cleaned the tar form his hands and fed Ben.

He was sitting in the lorry, resting his back against the low sides when Mary O'Leary appeared with his dinner: a plate piled high with roast meat, roast potatoes and vegetables, Yorkshire puddings and lashings of gravy. He was starving hungry and wolfed down the food, meat and all, saving just the one slice for Ben. He'd given up eating meat – even in countries where it was the main ingredient of all meals because he'd come to find the taste unpleasant – but was glad of it after the day's work.

Bingham had wasted days during previous investigations, but always with the hope that tomorrow would prove more fruitful. If he was to be stuck with O'Leary this wouldn't be the case. Other than snapping orders and boasting about how much he'd conned out of naïve pensioners, the man had refused to engage in conversation, considering it beneath him to converse with a dossa.

The meal had been satisfying and driven him to the edge of sleep. Bingham was wondering whether he had the will to find a local pub close by and wash the food down with a beer when Martha O'Leary appeared with a can in her hand.

"Amos says you play the flute," she enquired, handing Bingham the can.

"Yes, I've played since I was a boy."

"Would you be playing Country music?"

"What was it you had in mind, Mrs O'Leary?"

"I'm very partial to Patsy Cline."

"My hands are raw from the day's work. I can't be sure of playing the notes as clean as I'd wish."

"We love a singsong."

There was a flirtatiousness in Martha O'Leary's manner: a device for getting her own way, no more. She was a short woman, dressed in a style that reminded Bingham of the fifties and the aunts of his childhood. The traveller's wife suggested the pop stars he'd adored as a boy: Susan Maughn and Connie Francis among them. Flared skirts and wide belts with hair piled and lacquered. Martha's hair was dyed a shade between auburn and red, heat-curled and sumptuous. She'd slashed a bright red lipstick across her mouth and her eyes were surrounded by layers of black mascara.

If he played, she'd drink and sing; and if she drank and sang, Martha O'Leary would talk. He'd played his flute in a folk group at university and his ear for a tune, despite encroaching deafness, was good.

"I'd appreciate a glass for the drinking, Mrs O'Leary. I've never found a can to be satisfactory," he said, "and when you fetch it perhaps you'd ask your husband for my day's wages. While you're obliging me, I'll warm my flute."

His speech was calculated to appeal to a woman who, he judged, lived in a world where men ruled, where their word was law. This woman spent her days looking after husband and family. No one asked what she might want to do with her life; it wasn't part of the culture. But the house was hers and the evenings, and this was her moment to take centre-stage and shine.

Martha O'Leary looked over her shoulder towards the trailer and then back at Bingham, as though she had something to say Amos wouldn't want to hear; but she was silent, merely smiled at Bingham, turned and went for his glass.

Country music wasn't familiar territory to Bingham, but he had a memory for tunes and as he took his flute from its case he recalled *Crazy* and hoped that Patsy Cline had recorded others he knew. He'd once bought a Hank Williams' LP because the girl he was courting at the time had taken him to see the film, *Your Cheatin' Heart*, and Bingham could remember more or less every song in the movie. It was to be hoped that Martha O'Leary liked them.

Evening was settling in when he began warming his flute by playing the *Londonderry Air*. It was an irresistible pull for the travellers even if they knew only the first two lines of the song. By the time Martha joined him, a large group had already gathered around Bingham. He treated them, as he had at The Albion, to a few more Irish ballads and then moved to *Just a Closer Walk with Thee*, which he remembered from a Chris Barber concert. Knowing that Country music often had a religious side to it, his choice was instinctive and proved to be fruitful: Patsy Cline had recorded the song and Martha knew the words by heart. She sang intuitively, her natural voice in sympathy with the words, and the camp listened.

Bingham watched the group become a crowd, first the women and then the men, and heard other voices join Martha's. What next – more Country religion? He wasn't sure until the song came to an end and his flute, as though taken over by a muse, moved to *I Saw the Light*. As he played, a young man climbed onto the back of O'Leary's lorry, a guitar in his hand; a chair followed, lifted on by a friend. The young man sat and began to strum, keeping a steady rhythm to Bingham's melody and trills.

Bingham knew he'd arrived. After a long and futile day, in the darkness of the camp he, too, saw the light. One of these people knew where Paddy Dolan's granddaughter had gone and they'd begun to trust Bingham, respecting the dossa's skill as a musician. Later tonight or perhaps tomorrow, one of them would talk to him.

Chapter Three

A BRIEF MOMENT OF AMAZEMENT

The young man's gaze held Bingham's eye as the crowd dispersed. It had been a good evening and the two musicians smiled at each other.

Bingham had eased back from his key role after a while. Nodding towards the young man, he'd suggested the guitarist chose the next song, and he'd proved resourceful, kicking in with *Jambalaya* and following on with *Hey Good Lookin'*. Bingham then took over with *Your Cheatin' Heart*, which brought Martha and the other women into the frame, and pursued the Hank William's repertoire with *Cold, Cold Heart* before beckoning in the young man who, very cleverly Bingham thought, gave a rendering of another Hank Williams number sung by Johnny Cash, *I Heard that Lonesome Whistle*, before *I Walked the Line* and *A Boy Named Sue*.

Both pleased with the evening, neither spoke for a while but sat in that quiet camaraderie enjoyed by men who have achieved something satisfying together. It was a brief moment of amazement, Bingham decided: in his case brought about after a fruitless day, in the young man's because he'd accomplished what, for him, was unusual.

"Is it the women who usually take over?" he asked.

"Yes. They enjoy singing and the men aren't too bothered ... but they like Johnny Cash ... and Hank Williams."

"I'm Michael Joyce ...?"

"I know. The men have already found that funny."

"And you?"

"Noah – Noah Flanagan."

"You could go far with a name like that."

"Are you trying to be funny?"

"No, no," replied Bingham, not wishing to antagonise the young man, "It's a name with a ring to it and your guitar playing's exceptional. Have you had lessons?"

"No."

"Then it's gift."

Noah looked at Bingham, uncertain as to what he was about, as though praise should always be treated with suspicion. Bingham knew what was going through his mind and waited. Noah flicked a cigarette from the pocket of his jeans but made no attempt to go. He pointed the pack towards Bingham.

"I gave up long ago – but thanks."

"All of us are smokers here. It's part of the culture."

"Along with the fighting?"

"You know about that?"

"I've heard. It won't do your fingers any good. You're needing to be careful. You have a gift. Treasure it. Do you get any chance to play off camp?"

"Sometimes – down at the local pub. They don't seem to mind us down there. The landlord's a decent bloke, reckons we're cleaner than some of his regulars."

"They're folk clubs, you know. They'd welcome someone with your talent."

"I'm not sure me da would like that. We don't have much to do with the Gorgias."

"You go in a group, do you?"

"Yeah."

"Youngsters of your age need each other's company. It's a good thing?"

"It's only the men go."

"The girls aren't allowed?"

Was it a question too far? Bingham caught Noah's sideways glance and the narrowing of his eyes, but it may simply have been the cigarette smoke.

"It wouldn't be right."

"The mothers keep their eyes on their daughters?"

"We look after our girls. They're not like the Gorgia women."

"It'll be one of your own you'll be marrying?"

"Ah – too right."

"Anyone in particular you've your eye on?"

"I'm not ready yet. Having a girlfriend means you've got to call her every day, buy her presents, pay for everything and if I end up not liking her and couldn't make her hate me, I'd have to propose."

"Once you've asked a girl out, you're committed?"

"If I went out with one of our girls more than three or four times the families would say we were 'going steady'. After a month or so I'd be expected to ask her to marry me. I'm not ready for marriage – not yet. I'll have to satisfy myself with the Gorgia girls."

"And it's the same for your girls?"

"What d'yer mean?"

"If they went steady with a man, they'd have to marry him?"

"No decent girl would do otherwise."

"How do the girls feel about that?"

"They learn to do as they're told ... We don't go around doing what we like. We do things the traveller way."

"It's likely, then, that you'd fall for a girl you knew – one you'd met at one of the camps?"

It was a stupid question and Noah's face said he thought as much. Bingham was only a dossa. What more could you expect, even from a Dublin man? Bingham didn't mind. It wasn't in his interests to seem too bright, but he had to steer the conversation around to Paddy Dolan's granddaughter.

"If you marry young, I suppose your families are large?"

"Four or five at least."

"And yet Mr O'Leary only has the little girl – Mary."

"Martha has the four. There's the toddler and Tommy, who's older than Mary – he was singing tonight – and ... and Lizzie."

"I've yet to meet them. Is Lizzie the oldest?"

"She was."

"You mean she's dead?"

"She might as well be."

"What do you mean?"

"Nothing! It's our way. It's not the concern of a dossa."

Noah looked at Bingham, ire in every line of his face and body. For a moment, Bingham thought the young man was going to thump him; but Bingham's old eyes must have seemed harmless enough because Noah's anger abated as quickly as it had risen.

"You don't want to go on asking too many questions, Mr Joyce. You'll be getting yourself into trouble," he said, and added, almost apologetically, "... You think we might play again tomorrow?"

He jumped from the back of the lorry and lifted his chair off after him. Noah had ended their conversation.

"That would be good. Bring any of your friends along who play," Bingham called to the guitarist's back as it disappeared into the darkness, which was lit only by the lights from the assembled trailers, "And don't forget what I said. You have a gift – nurture it."

The night had settled in. Ben was snuggled on one of the blankets, out of any draughts at the far end of the lorry. Bingham thought over the conversation he'd had with the youth. His memory faded quickly these days; it was a struggle, sometimes, to hold onto thoughts. By tomorrow morning, he realised he'd have forgotten many of the tunes they'd played that evening. The strange thing was that something often called up memories from his past. A tune he'd long forgotten, conjured perhaps from a remark of the young man's, came into his head. He put the flute to his lips and began to play *Stop the World and Let Me Off*. It was a Patsy Cline song, but where had he heard it before?

"Will yer shut the row?"

The voice was O'Leary's calling from the doorway of his trailer. Bingham heard a woman's voice mumble something, and the door was slammed shut. Ben stirred, ears pricking, and looked towards the trailer and then at Bingham.

"Do you fancy a last walk, boy? Come on, let's take a look around."

He lifted the dog down from the lorry and the terrier padded along by Bingham's side. He'd never walked

Ben on the lead, neither he nor the animal liking the idea of a leash.

It was another warm night and the smell of stale food and other droppings was pungent on the air. Unattractive though the toilet block was Bingham had no choice but to attempt to use it. He hadn't seen any of the travellers in the place and assumed they all had their own facilities. How long the toilets had been in their present state Bingham had no idea. It was a private site, and no one seemed inclined to keep it clean.

After he'd brushed his teeth and splashed his face with water from a dripping tap, Bingham decided to look at the other trailers. He knew he'd have to be careful: strangers were clearly not welcome, especially nosey ones. Most of the trailers looked well kept up; the few that showed signs of age were washed clean, and there was the odour of fresh paint. Here, there was pride and money. Having seen O'Leary earn almost two thousand pounds that day, Bingham wasn't surprised.

Lights were going out in the trailers. Bingham heard the muffled sounds of 'goodnight' and the end of the day shouts from children. Occasionally a door opened, and someone threw something outside: perhaps an unfinished drink, perhaps the remains of a meal.

The previous night he'd noticed several dogs skulking about the camp. One or two were tied to their owners' trailers with pieces of string, but most seemed free to roam. They were all ragged-looking animals, all intent on sniffing out any scraps they could find

He wondered what Lizzie O'Leary made of this life. Did she question it or, like Noah, accept it as 'our way'? He'd worked with young people for forty years and realised there came a time when they and their parents – but no, he'd no reason to suppose any such thing.

Of course, Lizzie O'Leary had never reached this site. She'd disappeared somewhere along a canal towpath in the Midlands or, possibly, further afield in London; but undoubtedly someone here knew her. Travellers must meet up quite often: Bingham sensed there were strong family ties throughout their community.

Mingled with Noah Flanagan's anger there had been disappointment and fear. If he knew more than he was saying, what was it he was withholding? Had it been a coincidence that O'Leary moved his family nearer London or merely that he'd done what he intended despite his daughter's disappearance?

Bingham, as often on a walk, had forgotten that Ben was at his side, stopping for the occasional sniff but always close at hand, and so the barking, angry at first and then expressing pain, startled him. One of the travellers' dogs, a Lurcher, had rushed out at them from beneath a trailer. It had made straight for Ben, snapping down at the smaller dog's neck. Somehow, Ben must have avoided the Lurcher's jaws and sprung to the side because when Bingham's attention was drawn to the ensuing fight it was the larger dog that was bleeding from one of its front legs. They circled each other, the intensity of the barking by both dogs becoming virulent in tone. The Lurcher held its position, turning only on the spot and clearly in pain, while the terrier ran around, contributing most to the din.

Doors opened, voices yelled, and Bingham felt the presence of men about him. There was laughter and anger in their shouting as they egged on the two dogs. Bingham, who had an intense dislike of dog fights, was about to intervene by stepping in front of the Lurcher and calling Ben off, when the smaller dog leapt in and sank its teeth into the Lurcher's leg once again. At that, the traveller's animal ran off yelping and Ben, licking his lips, looked up at Bingham.

"Bloody runt!"

It was one of the travellers who swore as he aimed a kick at the terrier's head: a kick interrupted by Bingham, who grabbed the man's outstretched leg and lifted it as Ben ran clear. There was disbelief in the man's face as he tumbled onto his back in the mud: disbelief immediately followed by anger. He was a short man, stocky and packed with muscle and fat. He sprang to his feet, fists clenched, squaring up to Bingham. The men formed a circle enclosing what they saw as the two fighters: a circle that was broken suddenly by Amos O'Leary who burst into it and stood at Bingham's side.

"What the hell's going on?"

"It was your dossa's dog. He bit my hound. I'll pay him off and then kill the bloody animal."

"Is this right?"

O'Leary's question was fired at Bingham, who stood almost dumbfounded by the sudden change of circumstances, his one thought being to ensure Ben's safety and wondering how that was to be achieved.

"Ben's a Cairn. They're bred for hunting otters. Once they get a grip, they never let go. Your hound was lucky to get away with a bite. Ben could have taken his paw off."

Bingham turned to O'Leary, who was smiling.

"Ben was a feral when we found him. He's gentle enough now but got used to looking after himself. When the gentleman's Lurcher went for him, he acted instinctively to defend himself. I'm sorry I tipped you on your back, but I wasn't having you hurt my dog."

"Is that right?" yelled the stocky man.

"That's right!" O'Leary yelled back, "Are you making anything of it, and do I have to beat you stupid?"

The Lurcher's owner shot Bingham a glance that promised trouble if he found him alone and dropped his fists. He said nothing but shambled off through the crowd. Bingham called after him:

"Are you not going to see to your dog? The bite will need tending."

The man turned, decided against a reply and moved on. His companions dispersed sullenly, disappointed at being deprived of the fight.

"Take your dog and get yourself on the lorry. We've work to do in the morning."

"Thank you," said Bingham.

"Don't thank me. No one threatens mine – dossa or not – and gets away with it."

With that comment, Amos O'Leary shuffled Bingham aside and made his way back to the trailer. Bingham watched him go and saw Martha standing in the doorway. As O'Leary pushed by her, she threw Bingham a glance that expressed pride in her man.

Bingham lifted Ben onto the back of the lorry and wandered off to look for the injured Lurcher, without losing sight of Ben, but the dog had fled, no doubt licking his wounds somewhere safe.

"You'll be giving me yesterday's wages before we move off, will you, Mr O'Leary?"

The traveller set his eyes on Bingham, who had just downed another enormous breakfast, with a look that was one almost of admiration; it appeared that Amos O'Leary took to a man who stood up for himself. He counted out the forty pounds and nodded Bingham into the cab.

"It's Saturday today," he said, "and we'll be back that bit earlier."

He didn't say why, but Bingham supposed that the work might be scarce with the husbands around; and this proved to be so. One old woman welcomed the gritting of her driveway, an old man paid O'Leary handsomely for the repairing of a fence and another told the travellers to clear off: a rebuke that O'Leary took with a smile and as gracious a goodbye as Bingham had ever heard. There was no other work that day and by mid-afternoon the lorry was parked alongside the trailer.

"That'll be the twenty pounds for half-a-day's work," said O'Leary, his face challenging Bingham to demand more.

"You'll have no objection if I go into town, will you, Mr O'Leary?"

The traveller looked Bingham up and down as though suspecting the remark to be facetious, but all he said was "Keep out of Joe Barry's way."

Bingham had decided on the same course of action. All he wanted to do in town was find somewhere there might be a shower working.

"You'll be back tonight, Mr Joyce?" called Martha from the trailer.

"I'm not used to this way of life, Mrs O'Leary. I was thinking of using the money I've earned to buy myself a room at The Albion for the night. A soft bed and a shower would be nice," replied Bingham, knowing he'd need somewhere safe to leave Ben while he washed and shaved.

There was a moment's pause as glances passed between husband and wife, and then the former gave a nod.

"It'll be just fine having you here to play, Mr Joyce. Why not use our shower?"

"I'd be most grateful. It's been some days now since I've been able to change myself."

"Give us a while and I'll see to it for you."

"You've a way with you, Joyce. I'll say that. Tomorrow you can help the kids lug over the water you've used," said O'Leary, his tone failing to carry the sarcasm his words conveyed, and he strode off towards the other end of the camp.

Bingham had notice, without paying much regard, to the large churns of water that stood outside the trailer, and now he watched as Martha and the children drew off the water, which he guessed they must be heating for his bath. He knew he was being honoured, both for himself and Patsy Cline.

The inside of the O'Leary's trailer was a marvel to behold: family portraits hung in every spare gap on the walls, Wedgewood crockery lined the shelves, a bright green sofa was covered with yards of home-made lace and lead crystal glassware decorated the windowsills. In the centre of what Bingham took to be the lounge area was a large chair with curved armrests and beside this another armchair, lace-covered like the sofa. A mahogany drop-leaf dining table, French-polished to perfection, occupied the far end of the room.

Martha handed Bingham two towels and directed him through a small door at one end of the trailer where he found the bath tucked neatly into the corner of the small room. The water, though shallow, was steaming hot and he emerged less than half-an-hour later shampooed, shaved and shining with cleanness.

Martha had a kettle hissing and a teapot waiting. She sat at the table; her children gathered round her eyeing a cherry cake. It was the moment he'd been waiting for. If O'Leary would stay out of the way for a while, Bingham might get Martha talking. He'd noticed the family photographs and pointed to one as he sat down.

"You have a fine home and a fine family, Mrs O'Leary. Four children, I see – the same as my wife and me."

"You have a family, Mr Joyce?"

Bingham, realising he was on the threshold of revealing himself, backtracked rapidly, thinking of Lina as he trotted out the lies.

"I was referring to my first family. My misfortunes started with my second."

"Divorce isn't something we travelling people look upon lightly, Mr Joyce."

"No, it's not the most pleasant of undertakings."

"I can't think of anyone in my family who would undertake it under any circumstances. Travelling people marry for life," said Martha, inviting Bingham to sit down as she poured him a cup of tea, "Amos always likes a mug, but I think the tea tastes better from a cup."

"Wedgwood pottery, I see. You have a fine collection."

"My mother it was began the collecting. I've added to it as the years have gone by."

"She must be proud of her grandchildren."

"Now she and my da have stopped the travelling, we don't see so much of them."

Martha paused, overcome by a quiet sadness. Bingham could see her thoughts travelling the rounds and he seized his moment.

"I've met Mary, of course – she's the kind girl who brings my breakfast. And your boys are?"

"Tommy's the oldest and the toddler's Sean."

"Fine Irish names, Mrs O'Leary. I was partial to Sean O'Casey's plays when I was younger. Who's the other pretty young girl in the photograph?"

The pause was enough, and a mistake on Martha's part, allowing Mary to chime in.

"That's our Lizzie."

"I haven't seen her around, have I?"

"She ran away at Cottingley."

"Ran away?"

"That's enough Mary. I've told you ..."

"I'm sorry to hear that, Mrs O'Leary. You must be sick with worry. How old was she?"

"Lizzie's fifteen," chipped in Mary.

"I said *that's enough*."

"I've no wish to intrude on your grief, Mrs O'Leary. I can only hope that your daughter's found safe and sound."

"Ah, if that was all that mattered."

"May I have another piece of cake, Mammy?" asked Tommy, a well-built boy who looked as though he might run to fat later in life.

"Hmm?" replied Martha, gathering herself together, "Why, Mr Joyce, I quite forgot to offer you a piece."

Bingham accepted the large slice appreciatively. He could see Martha was on the point of explaining or denying.

"Do you have family on the site, Mrs O'Leary?"

"Yes, my sister-in-law's people. It's why we're here on this god-forsaken pitch. The council sites are better equipped but Amos likes the family around him. We try to meet up when we can."

With the children subdued and their mother withdrawn, Bingham knew he'd garnered as much information as he was to be allowed to know. It was a smidgen, but it might just be enough to offer him a lead.

Chapter Four

ARTFUL WITH A DASH OF DECENCY

Bingham bade his farewells and thanks just as Amos returned to the trailer. He eyed Bingham, as though suspecting Martha had been compromised but said nothing, his mind – Bingham decided – being elsewhere. Nevertheless, Bingham had to smile when he heard Martha call out:

"You'll be wanting to come to Mass tomorrow, then, Mr Joyce?"

"That's very thoughtful of you, Mrs O'Leary. I should be most grateful for the lift."

He smiled, but had he any reason to do so? What had he learned that was of any use to his search? He'd picked up the name of the site near Leeds where Lizzie had disappeared (something a policeman would have done when he first spoke to Paddy Dolan) and Amos's sister was at the present camp; but would she be any more likely than Martha to talk to him? On further consideration, Bingham thought not. Even if he could get the women talking, their men would step in.

He could, at least, wander the site and perhaps gain that sense of place he'd found so helpful in the past; if he recognised no one, they would certainly know him – the dossa who played the flute.

In daylight, Bingham saw that the site was bigger than he'd expected. At one time it may well have been a decent enough place. The trailers were arranged in a circle and behind each there was a small patch of ground that looked as though it might once have been a vegetable garden. On one or two of these patches lingered the remnants of sheds and heaped in most were the remains of old cars, rubbish and other scrap. The central area, where the trailers faced one another was roughly tarmacked and the home of a few barbecues that had seen better days. It was here Bingham found the children running in circles around each other in what resembled a game of tag.

Beyond the edges of the site he found horses tied to stakes bashed into the ground. Many of them were mangy-looking animals in need of a good feed and medical attention. Further into the surrounding forest, trees had been cleared and stacked and their roots dug out creating a field where several men were watching another breaking-in a fine-looking beast with a deep red coat and a long, flowing tail that twitched from side to side. Bingham was reminded of his many cats whose tails always jerked back and forth when they were annoyed.

The men looked at Bingham and Ben and passed one or two comments among themselves, but they did not speak. There was a sense of threat in the air, and Bingham realised he was out of his depth, asking questions, nosing around in a world he did not understand. It made him uncomfortable to realise his safety, should any of these men take a dislike to him, rested in the hands of Amos O'Leary.

He made his way back through the circle of trailers looking for the one that belonged to Marth's sister-in-law.

He had no expectation she would speak to him, but he felt that knowing her trailer would draw him closer to the reason Lizzie O'Leary had disappeared. These women must talk like any others, he thought; somehow, he must find a way of making them talk to him

It was in the central area he came across Noah Flanagan, who was leaning against one of the barbecues watching the children at play. Something about the young man was sheepish. Bingham saw that at once in the hang of his shoulders and in the way he averted his eyes as Bingham approached.

"Hi there, Noah, you'll be looking forward to tonight, I expect."

"I'll not be playing tonight. I'm off into town with the lads."

"Oh, I'm sorry to her that, Noah. I'd hoped we'd play together again."

"Some other time perhaps," replied the young man, shrugging his shoulders and slouching off.

Bingham watched the youth, but Noah never looked back and Bingham wondered why he'd changed his mind. Was it the fear of being associated with a dossa? What was the strength of the pull these older men, who clearly held Bingham in contempt, had over the youngsters? Since his set-to with Joe Barry, Bingham's apprehension had grown. Had the man hit him, Bingham would have had no means of defending himself. In all his travels across Europe as a young man, rarely had Bingham felt threatened or been in danger of assault; when he had been, Bingham found it possible to talk himself out of trouble, but talk wasn't an option now.

Among these people, defending oneself through fighting was a matter of honour. He'd read a book a few years before – probably Mikey Walsh's *Gypsy Boy* – where he learned that once a man raised his fists it was expected that the one challenged would fight, even if the chance of winning, or even remaining relatively unbruised, was negligible. It sounded to Bingham like a paradise for bullies, but who was he to judge. Had Noah been threatened?

He wandered on, deep in thought, towards the far end of the camp. The smell of cooking once again reached his nostrils and he glanced down at Ben, who was always excited by the odours of the kitchen. One or two of the women were cooking in pots outside their trailers over an open fire, while others could be seen through the windows bent over what Bingham supposed was a stove.

At home, Lina would be about the same task, the dogs would be hovering and the cats waking for their supper before setting off on their nightly prowl round the old farm. Bingham felt homesick, but he couldn't risk phoning Lina; his adopted persona was essential if he was to find Lizzie O'Leary.

"You'll still be playing will you, Mr Joyce?"

It was a woman's voice calling out to him, and Bingham looked up.

"You'll be Martha's flute player."

"And you'll be Amos's sister?"

"Theresa Dwyer," replied the woman.

Bingham held out his hand, but Theresa looked down and stirred her pot. She was a stout woman and shared her brother's mop of thick, black hair. When she looked up again and Bingham held her eyes, he also judged she shared his short temper. She was dressed for the evening, but over the bejewelled skirt and blouse wore an apron of the sort Bingham associated with his grandmother: it slipped across her shoulders and wrapped round the front, covering the whole of Theresa's clothes.

"Yes, I'll play whether there's anyone here to play for or not."

"There'll be the women and some of the men. They'll not all be going where young Flanagan's off to."

"Would that be The Albion?"

"And elsewhere, no doubt," replied Theresa.

She was obviously going to say no more but rather cast her thoughts to Bingham with a knowing look.

"Ah, the young folk, they are a worry," said Bingham, more in hope than expectation of an answer, but continued by way of encouragement, "I've had children of my own. Both my daughters were on the wild side when they were younger."

"Martha was saying you had the four."

"That's right, but none of them ran away, thank the Lord. Youngsters these days!"

"You'll be thinking of young Lizzie?"

Bingham withheld a smile. Always in women, he'd found the desire to confide. Whatever their background or culture they loved to divulge what they knew, believing themselves to be the possessors of knowledge denied to others. He'd seen it in his mother, in Lina and, later, in his daughters; he'd seen the same trait in women he'd met on his travels. Some might call it gossip, but Bingham preferred to think of it as an attribute, a desire to reach a consensus of understanding.

It wasn't always the case, of course. Martha had closed him down, but he had hopes of Theresa Dwyer.

"Mrs O'Leary mentioned her daughter, it's true," lied Bingham, "but the girl'll be back, I'm sure."

"There's no chance of that happening – none at all," replied Theresa in a tone that Bingham felt sounded crafty with a dash of decency.

"They always return," insisted Bingham, "Tomorrow, we'll pray for her and ask the Lord to return her to the bosom of her family."

"I tell you; she'll not be coming back. God help her poor mother."

"She's a kindly woman is Mrs O'Leary. She deserves her daughter by her side."

"You get caught up with the likes of Martin Boylan and you know what'll happen."

"This would be at Rushton End, would it not? It's a tidy way from here."

"Ah, and further than that now, I'm thinking."

"They'll be someone looking after her, I'm sure. They'll not see her come to harm," suggested Bingham, hoping for another outburst from the sister-in-law in whom Martha must have confided.

"Oh ah, she'll be looked after all right," Theresa Dwyer snapped.

She returned to her stew; the conversation was over for the moment, Bingham decided. Perhaps later, after the sing song, with the drink oiling her desire to divulge, he might learn more; but at present it was best not to acknowledge what he had learned.

Lacking the presence of the men, the singsong took on a more sentimental nature. When Martha had exhausted her Patsy Cline repertoire, one of the younger women, little more than a girl, began singing *Send Me the Pillow that You Dream On* and the night became Dean Martin's. Bingham found he knew most of the songs by ear. When he didn't, he improvised a few trills along the way. *Everybody Loves Somebody, Volare, On an Evening in Roma* and *On a Slow Boat to China* were sung with a wistfulness that made Bingham think of the lot of women in this society: not one of them had suggested they might accompany the men to the pub and not one of them had suggested the alternative his own daughters had been vociferous about, a girls night out.

Eventually, as the night wore on the women drifted back to their trailers, chatting among themselves, laughing, giggling and lightheaded from the alcohol they'd drunk. Martha carried her toddler, Sean, hurrying the other two before her.

"It's best they're asleep before their da gets home. He'll only rouse them up."

Bingham remained where he'd sat all night, his back to the small fire that still crackled and spat under Theresa Dwyer's stew pot.

"You'll not be wanting another helping, Mr Joyce? It's a shame for it to go to waste."

"Thank you," said Bingham, not because he was hungry but rather that he was hoping for further conversation.

Theresa handed him a large helping on a plate. The stew was a mixture of swede, turnip, onions and what he took to be rabbit; he hadn't tasted anything like it since he was a boy, and once again was reminded of his grandmother standing over the coal-fired stove in her kitchen, her face red with the heat.

"You must forget what I told you earlier, Mr Joyce: Martin Boylan's name's not for mentioning here."

"Where might he be, Mrs Dwyer?"

"I've no idea, but they'll all be meeting up soon at the Appleby Fair. I only hope to God he stays away."

"I take it he wouldn't be a favourite of Amos's?"

"I'm saying nothing against the lad. It's just gossip I'm passing on."

"But he was fond of Lizzie?"

"If Martha knew I'd even mentioned his name …"

"But you have, Theresa, and you may as well tell the rest of your story."

"He was always hanging around their trailer. He had an eye for the girls, that one, and he fancied young Lizzie. One night, Amos came back from the pub, wild as you like, and found him snogging with Lizzie on the doorstep. Amos went mad. He flung Lizzie inside and beat the living daylights out of young Boylan – swore he'd kill him if he ever found him near his daughter again."

"It was Martha told you this, was it?"

"Who else?"

"How old was this Martin Boylan?"

"Keep your voice down, for God's sake! He's a bit older than young Noah – about nineteen. We're not very hot on birthdays."

"I'll say nothing to anyone, Mrs Dwyer. You can rely on me."

Bingham's mind was made up; his only problem was how to go about carrying out the scheme that had been forming in his mind all night. To sleep on it would be a good thing. By the time they'd returned from church tomorrow, he would have fleshed out the skeleton.

Lina's mother being of a Roman Catholic family, Bingham was used to the pattern of the Mass; in his own way and despite his reservations he enjoyed the ceremony.

The church was a small one, tucked away in the corner of a village a few miles from Chertsey. Amos had "sussed it out" on their arrival at the camp.

"We say our prayers every night, Joyce," said Tommy, who Bingham sat next to in the back of the old BMW, which Amos had valeted to a high state of excellence for their Sunday morning excursion.

"I'm pleased to hear it," replied Bingham, smiling down at the rather plump, cake-loving boy who was dressed in his Sunday best: a short-trouser suit in grey with a pink stripe in the fabric. His hair was slicked down with what Bingham supposed was the modern equivalent of Brylcreem. The tie his mother had tightened round his neck over the spotlessly white shirt looked fit to strangle him.

"Do your children say their prayers, Mr Joyce?" asked Mary.

"They used to. Their mammy was very strict about that, but they're all grown up now and living away, so I'm not sure they still do."

The priest welcomed the family and those others who had come from the traveller camp – for the O'Leary's were not alone in their devotions – and ushered them into the church, where they joined the regular communicants.

There was no edge here, Bingham noticed: the Gorgias turned and smiled as the travellers took their places, shuffling along the pews and filling the church with the smell of eau-de-cologne that battled for precedence with the incense.

Bingham had always found the naturalness of Catholic services strange, and he put this down to the formality of the Anglican tradition. On one occasion, when he'd accompanied Lina to a Mass in her mother's church, he heard the priest pause in the middle of prayers to remind the congregation that there was a bingo evening in the church hall on the following Wednesday. Perhaps it was this acceptance of religious worship as just another aspect of daily life, much like cleaning the car or cooking the dinner, that appealed to travellers like the O'Learys.

Certainly, they came out of the service smiling and laughing with Mary dancing down the footpath to the gate.

"I love Mass," she said to Bingham when he caught up with her, "I love the service."

"You always know what's going to happen," chipped in Tommy, "It doesn't matter where you are, it's always the same."

"And the Gorgias don't look down on you there," said Martha, catching up with her children, "It's the one place we mix with them, where we don't feel different."

"I'll walk back to camp, Mr O'Leary," said Bingham, as the family scrambled into the car, "I feel like stretching my legs, if it's all the same to you."

"And what if it isn't?"

Bingham smiled; there was nothing he could say.

"I'm picking up some tar barrels this afternoon. You see to it that they're got ready for the morning."

"Sure thing, Mr O'Leary, I'll be back in time to give you a hand."

Watching the BMW pull away, Bingham thought to himself that watering down the tar for Amos O'Leary would be the last thing he'd do for the man – at least, for the time being. A few words with the priest now, and tomorrow he'd set off for the traveller site near Leeds.

Chapter Five
KNOWING LOOKS AND GLANCES

"You're leaving! Now there's gratitude for you."

Amos O'Leary was not amused. Bingham had decided, having downed another of Martha's hearty breakfasts, that he should pay his dues with a day's work and give Amos some notice of his intentions, however short. With this consideration in mind, he'd got as far as the quarry and shovelled in a load of the pink grit before he spoke to the traveller.

"You'll not get work with any of us. I'll see to that; you can be sure."

"Your wife's breakfast was more than compensation for the loss of a day's pay."

"She quite took to you, didn't she – Martha. You're the first dossa to use our trailer, I can tell you. And me stepping in when Joe Barry went for you – there's gratitude!"

Bingham could see the man was working himself into a frenzy, into a justification for landing Bingham a punch; above all, Bingham wanted to avoid a confrontation of that nature and his tone became even more mollifying as he offered O'Leary a compromise.

"I take your point, Mr O'Leary, and I'm certainly grateful for your kindness and that of your good wife. Perhaps we could split the difference with me giving you my labour until lunchtime, but I must be on the move by early afternoon."

It was all the traveller needed to take the high ground.

"You can stuff your time up your arse. There'll be no money coming from me this day, and you can make your own way to the fecking road."

With that remark, O'Leary climbed into his cab, slammed the lorry into gear and did all he could to run over Bingham as he shot away, grit flying in a cloud of pink dust. Bingham smiled to himself, relieved and ready for the next step on the trail.

Bingham had always considered himself to be lucky, and this proved to be the case on his trip to Manchester. Once he and Ben reached the M25, they were picked up by a lorry driver who was going the whole distance. Two stops – one for a coffee and one for a huge lunch – later, the driver dropped them at Rushton End Traveller Site.

"And the best of luck, mate – you'll find some funny buggers in there," he called out as he waved goodbye, his last remark echoing his conversation for most of the journey.

Bingham stood back and admired the site. This was council-run, and the approach was along tarmac roads with footpaths to either side. Some planner, doubtless with a sense of humour, had named the road Gypsy Lane. Streetlights were placed at strategic points, including the entrance, where a stretch of grass softened the appearance of the concrete sheds and wire fence.

As Bingham walked onto the site, he was met by an elderly man in blue overalls.

"Can I help you?"

"I hope so. I'm looking for a man called Amos O'Leary. I understand he has work on hand."

"You've missed him. He left – ooh, it must have been the best part of two weeks ago."

"Ah," replied Bingham, feigning disappointment, "That's a shame. I'm desperately in need of work."

"You know the O'Leary's, do you?"

"Yes. Martha has a fondness for Patsy Cline," replied Bingham with a laugh, "And young Lizzie has a fine voice. You should hear her singing ..."

"You won't be hearing her singing again – at least for a while, if not forever," replied the man, drawing in his cheeks as though suppressing a vital piece of information, which was what Bingham hoped.

"Why's that?"

"You're Irish, aren't you?"

"As near as you like to Dublin."

"I thought so. I can always tell. I can place an Irish accent to within a mile of where it comes from ... You're what they call a dossa, are you?"

"Since I fell on hard times."

"I'm Stan Brown. I'm the caretaker here," replied the man, rubbing the tip of his nose with the back of his right forefinger and looking carefully around, "She ran off."

"Who? Lizzie?"

"No other."

"But she was so fond of her parents. I can scarcely believe my ears."

"Believe them or not – that's what happened."

"When was this?"

"Just before they left the site."

"She ran off overnight, did she?"

"So, it would seem. Her grandfather's been up here looking all over the place, but he couldn't find her."

"That'd be Paddy Dolan?"

"You know him?"

"I met him once. He's a nice man and fond as fond can be of Lizzie. He'll be devastated. What can she have been thinking of?"

"Who knows, with these girls?"

"Did she go alone?

"Ah – now you're asking. Young Martin Boylan disappeared at the same time. I'm putting two and two together."

"And no one's any idea where they went?"

"If they have, they're not saying. She was only a girl, you know – what, about fifteen or sixteen? Mind you, they get married young, these gypsies."

"How did the young man's family take it?"

"It didn't seem to bother them too much – but they're a funny lot. Anyway, it's different for a lad. You know the Boylans, do you?"

"No, no, never met them."

"He might have some work for you. He's always busy – when he's not fighting, that is."

"Runs in the family, does it – the prize fighting?"

"Let's just say you wouldn't want to meet him when he's drunk. He'd pick a fight with anyone, would Tony Boylan. I'll take you over to their pitch and introduce you."

"Just before we go – what did you mean by 'I won't be hearing Lizzie's singing again, at least for a while, if not forever'?"

"I'll leave you to work that one out for yourself. Let's just say he was getting all he'd want at The

New Inn without tying himself down with a young girl."

"He was having an affair with a local woman?"

"These boys all know where the red-light districts are – never you mind! All the stuff you hear about gypsy men keeping their marriage vows for life is a load of crap."

"You don't like them?"

"It's my job, isn't it? I don't have to like the people I work for …"

"It helps."

"You see this site, don't you? You couldn't wish for better, could you? And are they grateful? Grateful be damned!"

The caretaker, his voice low, had built himself up into a quiet frenzy. He was a little man, his skin wiry and gnarled, and he almost hopped on the spot with indignation as he spoke.

Bingham looked around the site and it seemed pleasant enough to him. Each pitch had its own water and electricity supply and was fenced and gated, there was hard-standing for the family's trailer and a brick-built unit that Stan Brown referred to as a 'shed'.

"The sheds have a sitting room, kitchen, shower and toilet facilities. They've even got washing and drying facilities – and do you know, they complain like merry hell about the water metres?"

Bingham had leaned close to the caretaker, the better to hear his whispered imprecations, and was met by the little man's eyes, sparkling with anger and waiting for the question 'why'. When Bingham didn't ask, Stan Brown snapped out the answer.

"It's part of their culture, see. To them, water's a natural right and not a commodity. Water metres go against the grain of paying for what you get. I told 'em – fetch it from the canal if you don't like paying for it."

While understanding that the cost of processing water had to be paid by someone, somehow, Bingham found himself agreeing with the traveller's point of view. Wasn't access to clean water everyone's right?

They passed several plots with their own vegetable gardens and others where turf had been laid and shrubs and bulbs planted.

"I'm guessing you'll have a waiting list for this site."

"It's closed. They know when they're well-off … Mr Boylan, this gentleman would like a word."

His voice rose to a shout as Stan waved at a large man, dressed only in a vest and shorts, unloading turf from the back of his truck. He turned and gave Bingham a hard stare.

"I'm away to Appleby next week."

"The horse fair?"

"You know it?"

"By hearsay only," replied Bingham, "I've no experience with horses, but I can lay turf and plants blossom at my touch."

"OK. We've got a few days before we go. You can help me lay this lot. Twenty-five a day and meals," he said, before adding, "and we'll take you to the fair."

The suggestion of a smile crossed Tony Boylan's face.

"The name's Joyce," said Bingham, extending his hand ready for the spit and shake, "Michael Joyce."

He turned to the caretaker who was already making his way back to the gate, and called out:

"I'm obliged to you, Mr Brown."

Without looking round, Stan Brown waved his hand in reply.

What time remained of the afternoon was short. Bingham had barely unloaded the truck and begun raking the topsoil on the Boylan's pitch before the traveller, who had disappeared into the shed after issuing Bingham with his instructions, called at him to "clean up" for his evening meal. Bingham found water running and the electrics working in a central block comprising toilets, showers and large washing machines where, Bingham supposed, the women gathered.

A boy of about twelve brought his meal, placing the dish on the back of the truck and looking the stranger up and down.

"I'm grateful to you, lad. You're a fine-looking boy. I bet you can throw a punch."

"And take it," the boy snapped back, "My brother taught me to take a punch."

"That'd be Martin?"

"That's right. He taught me to take the punch and never mind the pain."

"You like your brother. I can see that to be true. I'd like to meet him."

"He's away, but he'll be back."

"Leroy, you come back here. Your coddle's getting cold."

It was a woman's voice calling the boy who shot off immediately leaving Bingham with his coddle: a dish comprising sausages, bacon, potatoes and other root vegetables in a thin soup. It was tasty – Bingham couldn't deny the fact – but the eating of meat was getting badly on his nerves and his stomach.

A dessert followed (jam roly-poly and custard), again brought by the boy. His stomach bursting, Bingham was placing the dish on the truck, hoping for further conversation, when he looked up to find Tony Boylan standing before him.

"You were asking about my boy."

It wasn't a question: the traveller's anger was apparent in his stance and his voice.

"Your lad was telling me how his brother taught him how to fight – to take a punch."

"You knew his name."

"Didn't the lad tell me," replied Bingham, not wishing to involve Stan Brown in any trouble.

"He says not."

"Then I must have come across it on my travels"

"Where have you come from?"

"I've been at a site near Chertsey."

"Who would you have met there?"

"There were the Barrys and the Dwyers, I remember,"

"Not the O'Learys?"

To lie would only involve Bingham in further deception, but he'd already indicated to Stan Brown that he was looking for Amos O'Leary, believing that would explain his presence at Rushton End where he knew the family had camped. Could he trust the caretaker to say little or nothing? Bingham decided he had no choice.

"That's right, the O'Learys – or someone of a similar name – were there."

"Amos O'Leary accused my son – Martin, that is – of running off with their daughter. We aren't on speaking terms with the O'Learys. Pack your bags and go."

"I'm sorry to hear that, Mr Boylan. I find work where I can. It's a dossa's life for me. I bear arms for no one."

The traveller turned away, his business finished, and Bingham, feeling he had no choice, lifted Ben down from the truck and moved off towards the gate where the lorry driver had dropped hm.

A closed society was a hard one to enter. He wondered whether the police investigating a crime had similar problems. How long had he been with these travellers? Bingham couldn't remember: one day seemed to run into another. It could only have been the previous Thursday he was playing his flute outside The Albion, he'd done a couple of days work for Amos followed by church on Sunday, and so today must be Monday. Five days only and yet it seemed an age: an age of silence and getting nowhere. All he'd learned was the name of a young man who had run off with a young girl.

"They don't even get on with one another," said Stan Brown, when he heard the Bingham was on his way out, "We've two sites here. The English Romany gypsies stick to one and the Irish to the other. I've never even seen the women talking, and that's saying something."

"You said that young Boylan had some kind of relationship with a girl at The New Inn. You don't happen to know her name by any chance, do you?"

"Which one?"

Bingham, his patience on the point of fraying, remained silent.

"Some of these young girls think it's what they call 'cool' to go with these gyppos … and some of them make them pay. You know what I mean? … There's Sharon Mottram – my wife knows her mother – God help her – and a friend of hers called Michelle something-or-other. They're always in there drinking. It's the age they are, my wife says."

"Thanks," replied Bingham, his mind settled as to what he would do. His only problem was Ben who may have lent authenticity to his role as a dossa but was now an encumbrance. He didn't trust anyone enough to leave him with and, besides, the dog would have been distressed, as he'd told Martha O'Leary. But luck was on Bingham's side: the kind of luck that had led him safely across Europe and, eventually, to Lina. Their eldest son, Paul, was a doctor and worked in a Manchester practice. Bingham was never sure quite where, but Lina would know.

The house of Paul and his wife, Marya, was within easy access of the M60 and close to the edge of the Peak District; in less than two hours Bingham was settled comfortably in their house, a watered-down whisky in his hand and his two grandchildren, Konstantin and Nikolai, on his lap.

Paul, following a hard day's work at the medical practice of which he was a partner, was not over the moon at seeing his father but his wife, who had always liked her parents-in-law, had seen to it that Bingham enjoyed a bath and a shave before settling in his son's favourite chair.

"Paul won't mind, and it's where the boys sit with him," she said with that faint Russian stretch of the 'o' and squeeze of the 'e' that Bingham always found attractive. "Why are you here, George?"

He told her, finishing the story as Paul arrived home and sat waiting for the evening meal the family always shared together.

"I don't know why you have to charge around in the way you do, Dad. Why not just enjoy your retirement?"

"Your father likes to help people, Paul. It's natural enough. I'll finish off the dinner while you talk. Are you joining us, George," said Marya, adding with a smile, "or are you full of coddle?"

"Full of coddle, I'm afraid, Masha, but thank you."

"Paul," said Bingham, adjusting the two boys on his lap and speaking as Marya closed the door behind her, "is there any chance I could borrow your car for the evening?"

"Are you insured to drive my car, Dad?"

"Yes, yes, I'm sure I am – 'any car that does not form part of a hire purchase agreement', is what it says."

"If you're sure. What do you want the car for?"

"I'd rather not say at the moment – and is there any chance of my borrowing some clean clothes? We're about the same size. I need to look respectable or, at least, clean."

The reluctance in his son's face was apparent, but before the family had finished eating Bingham was on his way to The New Inn at Rushton End, a distance of some fifteen miles.

The pub was packed but not yet heaving with life. Bingham could see a few travellers among the drinking crowd, but Tony Boylan was not among them. Bingham made his way to the bar where the barmaid, her low-cut blouse at the ready, gave him a smile and asked what he wanted. Looking at what was on offer – tasteless session beers from the large breweries – Bingham ordered a double whisky and water.

"Do you happen to know a young woman called Sharon Mottram?"

"Who's asking?"

"I'm looking for the daughter of a friend of mine, and I'm told that she knows Sharon or her friend, Michelle."

"You can take your choice, then. They're both sitting over there, done up to the nines and waiting for the action."

"Thank you," said Bingham, pocketing his small change from the ten pound note he'd placed on the counter.

The two young women were, as the barmaid had said, dressed for the evening: high heel shoes, make-up plastered in abundance, skirts up to their crotch, strappy blouses and fake leopard-skin jackets resting on the back of their chairs. They sat together at a round table in one corner of the bar, bent forward over their drinks, which looked like some kind of cocktail (a concoction Bingham disliked because he considered it destroyed the taste of the original spirits), talking in that intimate way women have while still being able to scan the room. As he approached, both young women looked up, their faces blank, their eyes wondering.

"Hello, may I join you for a moment?"

The women passed knowing looks and glances as Bingham pulled a third chair into place and sat at the opposite side of the table to Sharon and Michelle. He was conscious the barmaid was watching and that Michelle and she exchanged a smile.

"I'm looking for the daughter of a friend of mine. Her name is Elizabeth O'Leary and I'm told you may know her."

The looks and glances were exchanged again.

"Who says?" asked Sharon.

"Martin Boylan was the young man."

"You've spoken to Martin?" asked Sharon, obviously both startled and interested.

"He was mentioned to me by a mutual friend."

The knowingness appeared in both the young women's eyes for a third time, and Michelle managed to include the barmaid in her glance.

"We don't know nothing," said Sharon.

"Oh, I think you do."

"Who are you? Are you a copper? No, that's daft – you're too old."

"I'm a private detective," replied Bingham, by way of what he hoped was reassurance.

"So, you're getting paid to find Lizzie?"

"Yes."

"So, what we've got to say is worth something?"

"Yes – if you like to put it that way."

"Have you got a car?"

"Yes."

"Let's take a ride. It won't do me no good if they know I've been talking about them."

"Do you want me to go out first?"

"Why?"

"Well, won't they think it strange you walking out of here with an old man?"

Both women laughed: a hard, knowing laugh that rather chilled Bingham. These 'women' were only young, he thought, scarcely out of their teens, if that, and yet they were clearly used to picking up men in pubs and being seen to do so.

"They get used to that round here, dear, don't you worry," quipped Michelle.

Bingham drove, under Sharon's direction, to a small common, where he parked, screened by gorse bushes from the main road. It was still light enough for him to see the young women's face, but darkness was closing in and lent a shabbiness to their rendezvous.

"Is that what you really want – to know about Lizzie – or shall we get in the back?"

"I really want to know about Lizzie. It will be good to find her; good for her and everyone associated with her disappearance."

"You don't half talk posh. That's why I thought you were after a bit more than information. The posh ones always pretend it's about something else."

Bingham felt he wanted to ask this young woman why she took to the life she did. Sharon Mottram was clearly younger than either of his daughters and her way of living could only, in Bingham's view, lead downhill. She was, obviously, no druggie: Bingham had seen enough of them to know. He'd once chatted with a prostitute he'd met in a pub who told him she enjoyed the work. When he'd questioned the risks involved – there had been several murders at the time – she'd simply replied that that was part of the excitement. A friend of Lina's had told her that it was a way of getting back at men: "they think their screwing me, but it's me screwing them" had been her comment. A single mother he'd known at his Midlands school, and who the school knew was strapped for cash, always found the additional money for school trips in her own way; with her it was a matter of pride – prostitution before charity.

"How much?"

"Sorry?"

"You were miles away. How much is what I know worth?"

"It depends how much you know. If it leads me to Lizzie, the information could be worth a great deal. Let's start at fifty pounds, shall we?"

Bingham took the fifteen-hundred-pound roll of notes given to him by Paddy Dolan and flicked out two twenties and a ten; he did it deliberately, watching for Sharon's reaction. She took the money and stuffed it, ostentatiously, between her breasts.

"The little scrubber was gagging for Marti. She wouldn't leave him alone, but I swear to God he never touched her. He didn't have to, did he? He was getting all he needed."

Sharon smiled a contented smile.

"She kept pestering him to go away with her. She was fed up being a gypsy, she said. She wanted a different life. She reckoned they could get married and get a council house down south somewhere. She had relatives down there."

"They didn't go to Lizzie's relatives."

"How do you know?"

"It's my business to know. I'm a private detective. So where did they go?"

"Marti said they found a car the other end of the canal by the estate. The owner had left it unlocked. Well, if you're daft enough to do that in a place like this you get what you deserve, don't you? Marti's good with cars. He fiddled about under the steering wheel and off they went. No problem."

"Where to?"

"He said he drove Lizzie down to somewhere in Essex and left her with relatives. I swear I'm telling you the truth."

The account didn't agree at all with what relatives had told Paddy Dolan, who had no reason to mislead Bingham; and yet, Bingham felt at the time that the grandfather was holding back on all he knew.

"How did Marti explain to Lizzie why he was leaving her and returning to Rushton End?"

"He said he had things to see to. You don't argue with Marti."

"Did he intend to go back to her?"

"What do you think?"

"But he didn't hang around here long, did he?"

"His dad told him to clear off until things had died down."

"Were the O'Learys still here when he returned?"

"No ... I don't think so."

"But you're not sure?"

"No."

"Don't make things up to please me, Sharon: that's no help at all. Martin obviously had time to see you when he got back."

"He got back the next night. He came straight to the pub."

"How did he get back?"

"He came on the train and hitched back here."

"How long did he spend with you?"

"What's that got to do with anything?"

"A great deal: it's important to know when he went back to the camp and how long he spent there."

"We spent the night in his mate's lorry. He went back the next morning."

"And yet he wasn't seen at the camp again. How do you explain that?"

"How should I know?"

"He must have gone back that night, if he went back at all."

"What do you mean?"

Bingham remained silent. He had no wish to humiliate the young woman who had probably told him all she knew; but the trail led back to Tony Boylan and another dead end.

"I know where you'll be able to find him," said Sharon.

"Go on."

"He was always talking about the horse fair at Appleby. He loved horses. He's bound to be there, whatever."

"I hope you're right," replied Bingham, turning to the steering wheel and reaching for the ignition key. He'd heard of the Appleby Horse Fair: ten thousand gypsies and thirty thousand visitors. He supposed there might just be a chance of finding Martin Boylan among that crowd. It was, however tenuous, a lead.

"You sure you don't want anything else?" asked Sharon, a tone of disappointment in her voice that Bingham failed to understand.

"Yes, quite sure – but thanks anyway," he replied, refraining from offering the advice he was dying to give since he was sure it would fall on deaf ears, "But you wouldn't by any chance have a photograph of Martin, would you?"

Sharon looked him over as though doubting his sanity.

"On my phone."

"Can you show me?"

"I can send it to you, if you like."

"Send it to me?

"Well, you've got a phone, haven't you?"

Less than two minutes later, Bingham drove away from the common with a photograph of Martin Boylan in his jacket pocket.

Chapter Six

BEARING DOWN MORE AND MORE

And so, the following week, Michael Joyce, complete with flute and Ben, arrived at Appleby-in-Westmoreland.

Bingham had spent ten days with Paul, Marya and their two children, where he'd been joined, at the weekend, by Lina, who had left the farmhouse and animals in the care of their very good friend, Phil Bassett, seeing no reason why her husband should be alone in enjoying the company of their grandchildren. Paul was less than pleased with this invasion of his home, while being delighted at seeing his mother so unexpectedly.

Over their first coffee together on the day she arrived, Bingham relayed his frustrations to Lina.

"Why not speak directly to the relatives, Bing – or is that a silly question?"

"Instinct. If Paddy Dolan could get nothing from them, am I likely to? Besides, I doubt whether Paddy would give me their addresses. He was holding back on his thoughts and his feelings ... through fear or shame ... I'm not sure."

"You think the girl is all right, don't you?"

"I'll know more when I find Martin Boylan."

The lorry driver dropped Bingham in the middle of the village opposite The Grapes public house at midday on the Thursday. A dozen horses, washed to shining and groomed to perfection, were tied against the kerbside, crowded by a few visitors and munching in hay bags or gazing moodily around. The animals looked well-cared-for, unlike most of those on the site at Chertsey.

Bingham, thirsty after his hitchhike, decided to make his way to a side street pub before wandering up the Long Marton Road to Fair Hill where he'd been told he'd find the main traveller encampment.

"You don't want to hang around too long, mate. The place'll be knee-deep in litter by the weekend," was the last advice he received from the driver.

Bingham noticed that many local shops were not only closed but boarded up as he followed Bridge Street across the Eden. He paused and looked upriver. Where it passed The Sands, travellers were washing their horses ready for sale. They rode them into the river and washed their hides until they gleamed.

He found The Poacher's Pocket on a street that led him away from the town centre past the church of St Lawrence. Bingham pushed open the door and found himself in a large bar. Leaning against the counter were several men wearing only a vest to show off what in the young was muscle and, in the old, fat. Most looked grubby and all were unshaven. A few others sat at tables. To his left, Bingham saw a rather timid looking man sitting with his wife and daughter, a girl of about eighteen; one of the travellers was making a nuisance of himself attempting to chat-up the girl. The man looked up and smiled as Bingham walked to the bar and ordered a pint of Ullswater Blonde. It was the only smile he received, even from the barman. He looked around, found a window that overlooked the street and sat down, handing Ben a crisp under the table.

He wasn't sure why he felt so tired; after all, he'd done little but walk and play with his grandchildren for the past ten days. Perhaps, as Lina had suggested, he might be better off at home "taking things easy" instead of "charging around", which was his oldest son's expression. Perhaps, once he'd found Lizzie O'Leary, he would settle down.

"Would any of you fellas be knowing the Boylan family. It's young Martin I'm looking for. I hear he might be welcoming some help with the horses."

Bingham's question was met by silence; no one even favoured him with a stare. He took a deep swallow of the pale ale and waited.

The timid man with his wife and daughter had indicated that the traveller who was annoying them might move away. Eventually, the man did, begrudgingly. The bar seemed filled with an air of menace, quiet but nonetheless rather frightening. It was almost as if the men in the bar were waiting for something to go wrong, for something to annoy them, give them cause for complaint and a reason to lash out. One of the older travellers seemed to appreciate this and he and Bingham exchanged glances.

"Is it the Derry Boylans you'd be after?" he asked.

"That'd be the family. They were at Rushton End last week laying turf and planting the shrubs."

The man nodded but said nothing else. After a while, he drained off his beer and left. Bingham was hungry but there was no smell of food being cooked.

"Not today," said the barman, "Usually you'd be able to get a meal here, but not today."

He offered no explanation as to why and with a nod to the family who were getting ready to go Bingham drained his glass and walked out onto the street. He re-crossed the bridge, ignored the horse washing for the moment and headed north along the Long Marton Road, which was now closed to traffic.

Young travellers were racing up and down this stretch of road in traps, whips in their hands, urging their horses on. From what he'd read while with his son's family, Bingham knew that this stretch was known as 'flashing lane', where the horses were shown off, or "flashed", to impress potential buyers.

Those already up for sale were roped to railings that bordered one side of the road and the visitors were pressed in between them and the hazards of the lane. Making his way towards the hill, Bingham was obliged to push in through the crowd to avoid being run down by the traps. He lifted Ben into his arms to protect the dog from the feet of the crowd. This was the travellers' fair and though outnumbered by visitors they dominated proceedings and highways.

Bingham didn't mind the fact: the fair was a tradition worth preserving, and his attitude was that people visited at their own risk. He did object to the litter, however – now ankle, if not knee, deep.

Skirting round to his right as he reached the brow of the hill, Bingham made his way into the huge expanse of traveller and gypsy trailers and caravans. It was an awe-inspiring sight. Normally these people were met in small, often family, groups; here, they stretched in a raggedly fashion across the hillside.

Bingham had no other plan but to attract attention to his search for Martin Boylan, hoping that someone would point the young traveller in the direction of a dossa who might be useful with horses. Not that Bingham was even familiar with horses, but it seemed to offer the most likely chance of work in Appleby.

Among the modern trailers were the traditional gypsy caravans and Bingham couldn't but admire them. Often, children sat on the steps of these, and whenever a tourist stopped to take a photograph the children would hold out their hands, palm upwards. The value of their celebrity status was recognised from birth, he thought.

There were market stalls offering the work of craftsmen and craftswomen, pottery, weaving and traditional gypsy wares among them: pegs, wooden flowers dyed with the juice of berries, baskets for a variety of uses (fruit, bread, fish, coal, kindling and laundry), skewers, brooms, mats, carpet beaters, dolls' house furniture and – Bingham noticed with a smile – skeps. In a moment of absentmindedness, he bought one.

There were also fortune-telling booths and catering stalls providing delights such as gingerbread men for the children as well as the modern burgers and chips, cider and beer. Bingham, past lunchtime and hungry, looked and found a veggie burger; it fell apart in his hands but was better than nothing. What he didn't eat, Ben cleared up from the grass.

The long, riding coat together with the fedora and his unshaven appearance marked Bingham out from the crowd of sightseers as did his question at every likely trailer he came across.

"Would any of you be knowing a Martin Boylan? I'm looking for work with the horses."

It was a long shot, but Bingham knew the power of gossip, having been on the receiving end of it several times during his working life, and was not unduly surprised when eventually his shoulder was tapped. It was the older traveller from The Poacher's Pocket.

"You'll be most likely to find the man you're looking for down at The Sands later this afternoon."

"Thank you."

"It's no trouble. If you're wanting the father, Tony's over there on the far side of the hill."

"I spoke with Tony only last week. It's the son I'm after."

"I'll be seeing you then."

Bingham offered his hand in thanks and it was taken in a firm grip, a grip matched by the direct look in the traveller's eyes, a look that suggested Bingham might need to watch his step.

As he walked back down the road, expecting to find a pub where he might get a decent lunch, Bingham was overcome, once again, by a feeling of exhaustion. Perhaps being with the grandchildren for ten days had taken more out of him than he realised; Bingham wasn't sure but rested himself against a stone wall that protected one of the houses along the road from traffic and traps.

The young men were still whipping along, bare chests glistening with sweat and water, heads high, giving way to no one. Some would yell in protest as they were photographed, but most looked askance at the impertinence. The horses they hurried on cantered impressively, their manes blown in the rush, their tails flicking from side to side. There was talk of these animals being maltreated, but here, for this moment, there was harmony between man and beast.

The crowd at the water's edge was large: some stood and gazed, others sat, while many families picnicked on the riverbank, tablecloths laden with food spread between them. Bingham looked up at the bridge he'd crossed earlier in the day; it was packed with visitors leaning over the parapet.

There were half a dozen horses in the river being washed and an equal number on the dry bed that edged the bank, while more waited their turn on the causeway, where two RSPCA officers stood watching.

The sun shone down from a cloudless sky; by mid-afternoon it would be very warm, and Bingham could see that those horses in the river would appreciate the cool water while those tethered by the roadside would need shade.

He looked around, checking faces against the one Sharon had sent to his phone, although by now he could have picked out Martin Boylan across a crowded room.

The men on the horses were, of course, not only concerned with cleaning the animals to present them for sale; part of the whole business was embedded in the cult of the stud – not horse, but man. Muscles and bravado were the order of the day as young men showed themselves off to potential future brides and the older men strove to establish their right to command. As the horses were ridden into the Eden, each had its head ducked under the waters, ducked and raised before the rider slid from its bare back and began the process of washing their steed.

Bingham knew this from what he'd read – but it was apparent, anyway, from what he'd seen at Chertsey when Joe Barry threatened him, in Amos O'Leary's manner at home, in the public house when the young woman had been pestered – that among travelling men, their manhood was central to their existence and identity.

He heard the screams before he heard the neighs of the terrified horse, and Bingham walked quickly to the causeway. A rider was in the river, a man in his middle years, burly in weight and aggressive in manner. The horse under him, whose flanks he gripped tightly with heavily muscled legs, reared up and it was all the man could do to hold the animal in place. The expression on his face showed vicious determination: there was no way he was to be humiliated by a horse. Command and conquer was in every muscle of his body, every line of his face, in the tightly drawn mouth and the anguished eyes.

It was clear to everyone that the horse was frightened of the flowing water. A decent man, a man possessed of any scrap of kindness, would have calmed the animal and ridden it quietly out of the river, but the traveller's manhood was at stake; he either beat the animal or lost face. With a brutality Bingham had read about but never witnessed, the man wound the halter rope round his hands, tightened it about the animal's nose and forced the horse's head down further and further.

The river was deep where the two fought – the man for dominance and the horse for its life – and so the beast's legs were held by the pressure of the water. On land, it would have stood a chance, while the man would have stood none, but trapped by the river and the traveller's weight the horse struggled in vain against its aggressor.

Screams from the horrified families only added to the awfulness of the situation: forcing the man on in his determination, panicking the horse until its ears could hear no more.

"For Christ's sake do something," Bingham yelled at the RSPCA officers, knowing that he, an old man whose real strength had long gone, had no chance of reaching the horse in time to save it.

The two men looked bewildered and stood amazed. The horse vanished beneath the surface of the Eden. The yells from the crowd grew louder and more insistent.

"Get it out!"

The travellers along the river's edge began forming a human chain in order to reach the horse. Bingham, more in desperation than hope, ran down the causeway. As he reached the water's edge, he felt a hand on his shoulder. A young man passed him and waded out into the deeper water, swimming and splashing his way towards the horse and rider. When he reached them, he pulled strongly at the man's leg and tugged him from the horse's back. The animal's head was yanked to one side, until the youth brought his fist crashing down onto the horseman's face, forcing him to release the halter.

The horse reared, its front legs threshing the surface of the river, and struggled towards the causeway. Eventually, it gained the shallow water and raced up the causeway into the town, scattering the crowds in its flight.

"That poor horse!"

"You could see the terror in its eyes."

"He couldn't handle it."

"It's ruined the fair for everyone."

Bingham wasn't sure who was shouting louder – the travellers or the visitors – but everyone's anger was directed at the vicious horseman who the youth was dragging from the river. His right fist never stopped pounding the man's head until they reached the causeway, where he ducked the rider under the water and held him there until bubbles spluttered to the surface. How much water the man swallowed Bingham was unsure but when the youth released him the horseman collapsed on his face apparently more dead than alive.

"He'll live," cried the youth, looking around him.

"Thanks," said Bingham, offering his hand to the young man.

"It was more than a pleasure. I could see what you were about but knew you wouldn't stand a chance. He was an idiot, trying to prove he was a hard man."

"I'm George Bingham. I believe you're Martin Boylan. I've been looking for you. Can we talk?"

"How ...?"

"Privately – there's a pub across the road."

Settled comfortably in one corner with a pint each (Bingham a Marston's bitter and Boylan a Foster's lager) and with Ben lapping water from the bowl provided by the landlady, the two men looked each other up and down. The youth, whose vest and trousers were being dried by the landlady, sat in borrowed clothes, still flushed with his success. He was a good-looking lad by any standards, and Bingham didn't wonder that the women and girls were attracted to him; but looks meant little to Bingham when it came to judging people. Amos O'Leary had the looks, apart from his beer-belly, and the charm, but he wasn't the man you'd trust to lay a new driveway.

"I'll come straight to the point, son, before this place gets crowded ..."

"How did you know who I was?"

"I've seen a photograph and was told you'd be down at the river this afternoon. It was pure chance you'd also be the hero of the hour … but I'm the last one to look a gift horse in the mouth and bumping into you after so long a search is a gift."

"What are you talking about?"

Bingham remained silent.

"Who gave you a photo of me? Who told you I'd be down at the river?"

Bingham looked at his watch. It wasn't the crowds that bothered him; it was one part of the 'crowd' in particular. He and Boylan would have been seen to enter the pub.

"I'm looking for Lizzie O'Leary, and you were the last one to see her alive."

"What do you mean?"

It was a foolish question, and the young man knew it: he was playing for time, trying to organise his mind. Bingham waited, and Martin Boylan, annoyed and at a loss, repeated it

"Have you been in touch since you dropped her off at her relatives?"

"No … I don't know what you're talking about."

"Doesn't that seem rather strange to you?"

"I don't like this. I don't like it at all."

He was rattled, and that was good: Bingham needed him rattled.

"I've been asked to find Lizzie …"

"Who …"

"By someone who is worried that she has disappeared from the face of the earth."

Martin Boylan stared at Bingham. The older man could see the youth was wondering who the hell he was. He continued, without remorse since time was short:

"You stole a car and drove Lizzie down to north London – possibly Essex. She hasn't been seen since, and no one's heard from her. You understand where that puts you, should the police get involved, don't you?"

"I dropped her off with her relatives."

"They say you didn't."

"Then they're liars!"

"Or you are – that's how the police will see it. They'll be traces of you both in the stolen car."

"This is nice! One minute I'm a hero and the next I'm ..."

Bingham looked at his watch; they'd been in the pub for twenty minutes, and time was running out. Bingham knew Boylan wouldn't offer the information without being put under pressure: travellers didn't trust anyone outside their own community. He also knew they'd do anything to avoid being caught up with the police.

"Was she in love with you? Did she fancy you?"

On edge, put him on edge. Martin Boylan smiled. Bingham knew he couldn't help himself.

"Did you assault her? She was underage, you know."

"I never touched her!"

"I was told she was 'gagging' for you."

"Who said that? Who's got it in for me?"

"At present, no one. At present the police aren't involved because no one in your community wants them involved. That's why I'm asking the questions. Where do these relatives live?"

"If you've spoken to them, you must know that."

"I didn't say I'd seen them, let alone spoken to them. I was told they'd denied ever seeing Lizzie and that you never dropped her off where you claimed."

"Is it her dad doing this – hey? Amos O'Leary – he's got a lot to answer for."

"No, it isn't Amos who asked me to find his daughter."

"I'm not surprised," was the youth's reply, more assertive, surer.

"All I want from you, Martin, is the address where you claim to have left Lizzie. I'll look into the rest. If you're innocent, you've nothing to fear."

"It's not that simple."

"Are you telling me you promised to join her?"

It was intuition that drove the question; without acknowledging them to himself because he hated pre-judging a situation, Bingham had already come to certain conclusions. Pushing the young man now would put Bingham in the driving seat: guilt was written all over the youth's face.

It was at that moment the two police officers entered the pub. Bingham rose immediately, smiled and shook their hands.

"I've been expecting you," he said, "Can I get you a drink?"

"We're on duty, sir."

"Perhaps a coffee?"

He was familiar with them. Perhaps they were old friends? Bingham looked at Martin Boylan. The constables looked at each other, down at Martin Boylan and then at Bingham.

"That would be good. Thank you. You'd be Mr Boylan – is that right?" asked the policewoman, turning to the youth.

"Yeah, that's me."

He was ashen; not only the colour but also the strength seemed to have drained from his face. Bingham watched from the bar as the coffees were prepared. This might just be enough to convince him. Bingham took the coffees over with another pint for Martin Boylan and then sat to one side, waiting.

It didn't take long: a description of events was all they required – that and an address should they press charges. Bingham confirmed what the youth had said and gave his name and address.

"He's an heroic young man," he said, "Everyone else just stood around – including me. If it hadn't been for Martin, the horse would have been drowned. Is it safe?"

"It was chased by a group of the travellers. But for them, it could have caused havoc. They calmed it down. It's got its mouth in a nosebag now."

The police officer looked across at Martin before closing her notebook and rising to leave.

"Well done, young man," she said, tapped him on the shoulder with her notebook and gave him a smile, "It's a pity there aren't more like you. Goodbye, Mr Bingham."

Chapter Seven

DIGGING UP THE FAMILY HISTORY

"You said nothing."

"You mean about the stolen car and Lizzie's disappearance? Why should I? I'm hoping to find her before she's reported missing, but I've been looking for a couple of weeks now and I'm getting nowhere – nowhere unless you can help me."

"They'll not report her missing."

"No, but she needs to be found if she's still alive."

"You keep going on about her 'being alive'. Why shouldn't she be?"

"You tell me."

The youth spun round. One moment the hero, the next cornered as though he was a criminal. The borrowed clothes were ill-fitting, built for a fat man and hanging loose on Martin Boylan's lean-muscled body. Embarrassed by his dress and embarrassed by his predicament, he clenched his fists. But this wasn't a matter to be resolved by punching someone senseless in a hidden corner.

"You leave it to me," said Martin Boylan.

"I can't do that, and you know why."

"You're saying it's not Amos?"

"Yes."

"All right, I'll trust you, Mr Bingham, but God help you if you let me down."

"My concern is a young girl ..."

"She's a woman ..."

"No, she's a girl and I hope to find her safe."

There was another moment of doubt, another moment of indecision – to speak or remain silent – and then Martin Boylan whispered an Essex address in Bingham's ear before looking him up and down as though assessing the old man's chances in a prize fight.

"Thanks," said Bingham, "The landlady's waving from the bar. Why don't you get dressed?"

What little he'd obtained from Martin Boylan was all that was on offer, Bingham realised; but armed with the address, he might be able to annoy others into opening up. He must, at least, try before heading south.

He'd noticed Noah Flanagan in the crowd by the causeway. Noah was one reason he'd hurried Boylan into the pub. One thing at a time and then think on it was Bingham's way: he was too old to be hurried. What was Noah's attitude to Boylan? Where had the guitarist been when Lizzie disappeared? Apparently, he'd been at Chertsey when the O'Learys arrived, but Bingham wasn't sure that was the case.

Leaving Boylan to the landlady's attentions, Bingham left the pub and strolled across the road to the causeway. Speculation and self-righteousness were still in the air. Soon the story would find its way to the local paper and then the nationals. The *Mirror* would certainly make a meal of it. Whatever might be said against the newspaper, it certainly vented the anger of the crowd; it was just a shame the anger cooled without anything being done about its cause.

Noah found Bingham. He'd been waiting. Bingham could tell immediately by the anger in the youth's manner. Had he seen the man forcing the horse's head under the water? Had he stood, limbless, doing nothing? Had he lost his manhood when Boylan rushed forward? If so, it placed him alongside the rest of humanity. How many people did Bingham know who would have done what Boylan did? Not many, but that did nothing to relieve Noah's sense of inadequacy.

"You saw what happened?"

The youth nodded.

"We need to talk, son, and today rather than tomorrow."

Bingham had dropped the Dublin accent and Michael Joyce's manner, and this wasn't lost on Noah. Bingham wasn't sure whether it was surprise or anger that held the greater sway in the youth's face.

"My name's Bingham, George Bingham. I'm a private detective and I'm going to find Lizzie O'Leary."

"Amos won't like this. He doesn't like being taken for a fool."

"Where did he and you go that last night at Chertsey?"

"Where'd you think?"

"It's time to stop the nonsense. I've enough information now to bring in the police. Either you talk to me or you talk to them."

"Amos'll not like the police."

"That's of no concern to me. Now, let's find a quiet corner and have a chat before young Boylan reappears."

"I'm not scared of him."

"No, but you are envious of him and his way with women. And he's a couple of years older than you with muscles to show for it. You might take him on one day, but today's not the day – not if you want to whip him."

A short walk along Back Lane brought the two of them to the cemetery Bingham had noticed marked on a way sign. The sight of so many resting places seemed to have a sobering effect on Noah: the young find it easy to ignore the prospect of death but not when it's staring them in the face.

"Where did Amos take you that night? He didn't want you to play, did he? It was too much for him to see the women taking over, wasn't it? Women are OK, but in their place – right?"

"We went to The Albion. You can always pick up a Gorgia whore there. Amos said it was time I became a man. When we got there, Amos called the girls over. They were all tarted up – miniskirts and plastered with makeup. You know the sort of thing. One of them made a beeline for me. 'I think she fancies you, Noah', Amos said, laughing. She didn't waste any time. Her hand was on my thigh and then stroking my crotch before you could say Jack Robinson. The other men were laughing.

"We chatted for a bit. I don't know why. It was clear she was only interested in one thing. And then she grabbed me by the hand and hauled me out round the back of the pub. There's a common there, and condoms everywhere."

Noah laughed but it was a mirthless sound. He was obviously half-repeating a joke he'd heard.

"I think the place was used as a knocking shop – and a piss pot by the smell of it. She was pulling at my trousers and slobbering on my mouth before I rightly knew what was happening. When I didn't respond, she pulled my hands under her skirt and into her knickers … I had to go through with it, or I'd have been a laughingstock."

"You think Amos put her up to it?"

"Why else would she have been in so much of a hurry?"

"You're a fine-looking lad."

"I think it was a set up. She didn't ask me for any money. When we'd finished, she went back into the pub."

"And you?"

"I followed, didn't I? What else could I do? I drank myself silly."

"Why do you think Amos put her up to it?"

"I don't know."

"When did you last see Lizzie with Martin Boylan?"

"It was at Rushton. We left before Amos's family."

"And Lizzie was still there when you left?"

"What's that got to do with it?"

Bingham left the question hanging in the air.

"I heard Amos caught young Boylan with Lizzie one night."

"There was nothing to it. Amos beat the shit out of Martin Boylan. He wouldn't go near her again."

"And yet I'm told that it was Martin who took Lizzie from the camp."

"Who told you that?"

Used to being ignored himself, Bingham followed suit.

"Do you know where the O'Learys are pitched?"

"You're not going to find them?"

"Oh, I think I am."

"Amos'll kill you."

Bingham rose from the seat by the privet hedge and wandered among the gravestones. At seventy-three, he was aware of his own mortality. Death didn't worry him unduly: only its timing and its manner.

"How much do you hate Martin Boylan?" he asked, turning to the youth.

"Enough to beat him senseless ... when the time comes."

"And Lizzie – how much do you love her?"

Noah Flanagan shrugged, whether at the sound of the word 'love' or because he'd found its corollary, Bingham was unsure.

"I'll find Lizzie," he said, by way of reassuring the youth and, perhaps, intending to keep him onside and quiet.

"Do you know where she is?"

"No, but if you've anything else to tell me, I'll be here tonight, and I'd advise you to be honest with me ... You or Martin Boylan might find yourselves in serious trouble."

"I wouldn't hurt Lizzie."

"Maybe, and maybe not; but she's a child and someone – someone old enough to be responsible – abducted her ..."

"Abducted?"

"That's what it amounts to, whether you like it or not."

Bingham felt mean for bullying the youth, but only marginally: these people had messed him about, withholding information, closing the shutters. Whatever their reasons, whatever their culture dictated, they'd all been complicit in aiding her disappearance.

"Now," he said, "where can I find the O'Leary's trailer/"

It was only when he had the trailer in sight, having walked back through the village and found himself breathless on Fair Hill, that Bingham realised it was a long time since lunch. He bought another veggie burger, which also fell apart, and sat eating it while Ben had his tea and a long drink offered by the man on the stall. He then made his way to the O'Leary's front door, and Martha answered.

She looked Bingham up and down, anger and contempt apparent in her face. After all, she'd shown him friendship, quite unnecessarily, and he'd walked away without a word; there's gratitude for you. Bingham spared her the comment.

"If you're interested in finding your daughter, Martha, we need to chat."

She, like Noah, noticed the absence of the Dublin accent and the tone of Michael Joyce. Martha O'Leary favoured Bingham with a frown, and he explained who he was and his purpose.

"It's up to you. I'm on my way south tonight. So, if you've anything to say, say it now."

"What would I have to say to the likes of you? If my Amos finds you here, he'll ..."

"... Beat the living crap out of me? I've heard that before, today, from at least two other people, but assaulting me won't find Lizzie, and it's Lizzie you want to know about, isn't it, Martha?"

"Do you know where she is?"

"No, but I'm not far off finding her, and if you people hadn't messed me about ..."

"Is she all right?"

"I don't know, but I'll know by tomorrow night. Perhaps we can talk before Amos gets back?"

Martha looked about her, at the hundreds of other trailers and caravans spread across the hillside and decided against inviting Bingham into her home. There was a table set out behind the trailer and she nodded to Bingham to sit.

"Can I get you something to drink?"

Even towards someone you had no desire to sup with there was courtesy.

"A mug of that strong tea would be welcome."

When it was placed before him with a huge slice of walnut cake, Bingham's manner became more conciliatory.

"I was asked to find Lizzie, Martha – never mind by who, but you can guess, I'm sure – and I came disguised to your camp because I knew no one would talk with a Gorgia."

"My family didn't call the settled people by that name. To us, you were just the 'country people'."

"Before I move on, I just want to know what you think. As a mother, you must have your thoughts about your daughter."

"Are you of the faith, Mr Bingham?"

He couldn't lie, but the truth would be unpalatable to someone like Martha and he'd suffered enough obstacles placed in his way.

"My wife is a Catholic, Martha. We were married in the church of St Mary Magdalene in Ipswich."

This seemed to satisfy Martha. She took a sip of her tea.

"You love your wife?"

"Very much."

"O'Leary and I were a love match, you know. He was a handsome lad in those days – gorgeous, a square chin and muscles. I fell for him hook, line and sinker. Daddy didn't like him – said he was a chancer – but I was smitten and wasn't having any of it. We ran away together – not like they do now! Oh no! It wouldn't have done. I wouldn't have shamed my Daddy and Mammy like that. We spent the night in Aunty's trailer. We were in separate rooms, but it was enough – that very fact we'd been away together was enough.

"Daddy was furious but he had to agree to the wedding, though he said he wanted to beat O'Leary's brains out.

"We were happy. We'd go out dancing or sit together in the trailer Daddy bought us, cuddled up on a big chair we had. That's where most of the children started – on that chair. He was very amorous was O'Leary, and I couldn't get enough of him. We laughed a lot. He's not a bad man – O'Leary. He'd always be laughing and joking. He was the life and soul at parties. Daddy said I brought out the best in him, and he loves me – I know that to be true. We'll often snuggle up there now, once the kids have gone to bed … "

Martha looked at Bingham, who hadn't moved even to drink his tea.

"Why am I telling you all this?"

"You're worried about Lizzie," he replied, taking a gulp, at last, from the mug.

"You don't think she's gone off with that Boylan lad, do you, like they all say?"

"Is that what you think, Martha?"

The missing girl's mother didn't reply but took another sip of her tea.

"What kind of girl was Lizzie?"

"What do you mean?"

"Was she headstrong like you?"

Martha looked at Bingham and laughed.

"You're a sly one."

"Was she?"

"Yes! I hope to God she's safe. If any harm comes to her, Amos'll have blood on his hands. I swear it."

"Let's look on the bright side for the moment and hope it doesn't come to that," said Bingham, trying to sooth the mother. He added, against his better judgement, "I've spoken with Martin Boylan."

"You've seen him? Not here? Has he the nerve to come here?"

"Keep Amos away from him. There's nothing to be gained by violence."

"If he's touched a hair of Lizzie's head …"

"We don't know that he has, Martha. We've no reason …"

"O'Leary won't need reasons."

"Martha, Martha, calm down, if only for your daughter."

She looked at Bingham, suddenly quiet. Was it something in his voice or the soothing repetition of her name? Bingham wasn't sure, but he was granted a smile and finished his tea with a gulp. He had all he needed to send him on his way. It was early evening and Amos would be returning soon. He'd best be away.

He offered his hand to Martha, who took it begrudgingly but gave it a squeeze nonetheless, and then made his way back into town.

The following morning – after an agreeable overnight stay at The Royal Oak where he'd enjoyed grilled fillet of salmon with Dijon mustard and tarragon hollandaise for his supper – Bingham travelled south, hitching once again along the motorways that were nowhere to be seen when he was a youth. Hitching was safer then, of course, at a time when most of society's toerags kept themselves hidden in dark places; but Bingham had no trouble and was dropped off by a kindly Polish lorry driver in Colchester High Street.

He'd returned to Appleby cemetery for a short while in the evening, but Noah Flanagan had not turned up. Bingham sat looking out over the gravestones as the night drew in and tourists and travellers faded from the town centre, leaving only their litter to sully the attractive little place.

He'd wondered about contacting Lina and travelling down with her by train in fresh clothes but decided against the idea. He was absorbed in the search by now. Colchester wasn't far from Ipswich and a plan was forming, however lightly, in Bingham's mind. Besides, Ben disliked travelling by train – witnessing the dog's distress on a trip to Cambridge had troubled Bingham – whereas he would sit quite happily watching the road from the cab of a lorry.

He went first to one of the local Catholic churches. He wasn't sure why: much of what he did was arrived at intuitively rather than analytically. He found the priest at the housekeeper's direction and sat with him in a pew by the quiet of the nave.

"I know the family," the priest replied, after Bingham explained his purpose and chatted about the church in Ipswich attended by Lina when her mother had been alive, "They settled down here some years ago when the council offered them housing. When you're their age there's something to be said for having hot and cold running water on tap, a washing machine and a dishwasher. There's a car parked out front and they've a neat, little garden overlooking the countryside at the back."

"Do they travel no more?"

"There's a council site at Severalls Lane not far from here. They've relatives there."

"Do you know the grandfather, Paddy Dolan?"

"I've met him once or twice. He seems a stable chap. It's difficult for travellers these days. Their culture's breaking down before your very eyes. Councils are closing sites, and this means families get split up and they've no reason to trust us, have they? It makes it difficult when things go wrong for them. They won't register with doctors or schools for example ... But you didn't come here to listen to my woes, did you, Mr Bingham? It's Lizzie O'Leary you're after."

"Have you met her?"

"Once. The night they arrived she asked me to marry them ... You looked surprised, Mr Bingham."

"It was more an expression of concern, father."

"Well, you needn't worry. I could see she was only a child. I told her to go home to her family and get herself into school. I never saw her again. I was probably a little harsh, but these traveller girls do themselves no good running away."

"So, I understand. Can I mention your name when I go to see the aunt and uncle?"

"I don't see why not, unless they've something to hide."

The old priest had been more help than he might have realised. Why he hadn't pursued the matter, Bingham was unsure, but his very status in the lives of the travellers was another lever Bingham could use.

He found the address Martin Boylan had given him: a small bungalow in a block of similar dwellings, their back to open country, their driveways just big enough for the one car. They were neat-looking places as the priest had said, almost too neat to be real with their low, privet hedges reminding Bingham of another age.

"Mr Kinch is it?

"And who might you be?" replied Martha's brother-in-law.

"My name's George Bingham and I've just come down from Appleby where I've been speaking with Martha and her husband, Amos."

At the mention of Appleby and the names that followed, a woman appeared at the door. She looked, cagily, over the man's shoulder.

"You'll be Martha's sister, Margaret, will you?" asked Bingham.

She didn't answer but looked up at the back of her husband's head for a reply.

"Father Kennedy pointed me in your direction," urged Bingham, never one to save his ammunition.

The door opened, slowly but surely, and Bingham was asked to step inside. Margaret Kinch looked him up and down and Bingham smiled back. She was very like her sister: tiny and on the plump side with dyed, auburn hair but lacking the abundance of make-up Bingham associated with Martha.

"Will the little dog be needing a drink?" she asked.

Bingham had almost forgotten Ben, who hopped over the step and sat quietly on his haunches by his master's feet.

"Thank you," said Bingham, and he noticed Margaret Kinch smile, as Martha had done, at his manner of speech.

"How can we help?" asked the husband, who Bingham had heard mentioned as James.

"Is it possible for me to sit down," asked Bingham, not wanting to be ushered out of the door before he'd gained a secure entry, "I've come a long way this morning and my feet are old and tired."

James Kinch didn't smile, but Margaret did and gestured Bingham into their sitting room. It might have been Martha's trailer, so similar was it adorned: the sofa was bright red rather than green but covered with lace throws and the Wedgewood gave way to Crown Derby, but family portraits were hung everywhere, family portraits and posters of favourite singers and entertainers, while trophies stood on the mantelpiece and windowsills and several pairs of boxing gloves hung on the walls.

"I'll come straight to the point," said Bingham, once he held a cup of tea in his hand, "I've been asked by a member of your family to find Lizzie O'Leary – your sister's child, Margaret – and my search has led me to your door."

"We know nothing of the girl's whereabouts," snapped James Kinch.

Bingham looked the couple up and down, a practice to which he'd grown accustomed over the past few weeks. They'd both turned ashen and a subtle blend of embarrassment and hostility was in their eyes.

"But I know that's not true."

"Are you calling me a liar?" asked James Kinch.

"Yes, I am," replied Bingham, "God rest your soul."

Had the insult come from a bigger man, he might have been thrown out on the spot but Bingham, although nearing six foot in height, was of a slim build and his lean, open face offered no threat.

"Who sent you here?" asked Margaret Kinch, quietly and with a note of resignation in her tone.

"Why weren't you open with Paddy Dolan when he came to you?"

"Daddy sent you here?"

"No, Margaret, your father doesn't know what you've done …"

"We've done nothing …" began Kinch.

"Oh, but you have …"

"Nothing wrong," interjected Margaret, "Nothing but offered help to a girl in distress."

"You aided the abduction of a child."

"I don't know what you mean.

"Lizzie is underage, Mr Kinch. According to witnesses you received her here when she ran from her parents with a young man and you've since hidden her from her grandfather."

"We meant no harm," pleaded Margaret, "Lizzie was in a dreadful state when she arrived."

"As well she might be. Can you imagine what will happen when Paddy Dolan and Amos O'Leary find out what you've done? Let alone your sister, Margaret?"

"I think Martha half-guessed, to be honest," replied Margaret Kinch.

"Women have an instinct for these things?"

"Yes."

"You never told me that," yelled Kinch.

"I thought you wouldn't understand. Anyway, she never said."

If she had guessed, thought Bingham, it might explain her lack of open anxiety; it would also say a great deal for her acting abilities.

"That wasn't my impression, Margaret," he said, softly, "I think it's time to unravel the mess you've got yourselves in."

"I think you're right, Mr Bingham, it's time to be open."

Chapter Eight
THE SLIGHTEST HINT

"Are you telling me they knew all the time?" yelled Paddy Dolan.

"Yes."

"I can't believe this. Why didn't they tell me? They'll have a lot to answer for when I catch up with them."

"You were less than honest yourself, Paddy. You either knew or suspected more than you were prepared to let on."

"What are you talking about?"

"You were keen to keep things quiet, were you not?"

The traveller looked closely at Bingham. In a boxer the expression in his eyes would tell his opponent that the man felt he'd met his match.

"Do you mind if I sit down?" asked Bingham. "I've had a long and tiring couple of days."

It was true, and not just an attempt to relax the situation. Bingham had eventually more or less pummelled his way to the truth, whereas normally he relied on gossip, a slip of the tongue or someone's desire to clear their conscience. He'd also travelled the length and breadth of the country and done more walking than he usually considered necessary.

"Offer Mr Bingham a seat, Paddy."

Once again it was a woman who came to his aid. Paddy Dolan's wife had stood quietly when Bingham made his announcement but now she came forward, pushing gently by her giant of a husband.

"I'm Martha's mother. Kathleen is my name."

She led Bingham from the hallway of their bungalow into what was the sitting room. It was clear immediately that here the two old people sat seeing out their lives surrounded by their memories.

Bingham didn't sit. His energy was immediately restored by the sight of the Dolan's room. It could have been the inside of Martha's trailer or the Kinch's living room: family memorabilia arranged on every surface. In particular there were hundreds of photographs. Bingham smiled at Kathleen Dolan and she nodded back her permission for him to handle them. Traveller weddings, traveller funerals, baptisms and birthdays held central place amongst seasonal celebrations: Christmas, summer fairs, family get-togethers. Bingham recognized the O'Learys and the Dwyers among them.

"I didn't think you celebrated birthdays," he said, holding up a photograph of Lizzie blowing candles on a cake.

"That's O'Leary for you."

Kathleen Dolan moved out to the kitchen from where Bingham soon heard the hiss of a kettle and the clatter of china.

"You've a nice place here, Paddy."

"It's better for the wife now we're ageing, but I'll always be a travelling man."

"I wouldn't be without my home," replied Bingham, "My wife and I were lucky: we inherited Bob's Farm from Lina's parents.

"This place is ours – every stick and stone of it. A working lifetime bought us this house."

There was nothing sparse about the furnishings: the occasional tables and stools were either original antiques or ones reproduced by someone who knew their wood and their craft, the curtaining and throws were handmade, two Chesterfields enclosed the open fireplace at one end of the room and a sideboard Bingham realised was mahogany dominated the length of one wall.

"You know your wood, Mr Bingham," said Paddy Dolan, watching the man he'd asked to find his granddaughter running a hand along the surface of the sideboard and pausing at the decorative inlays.

"My father was a solicitor. He had a lathe in an outhouse where he'd go to relax when he got home. I learned a little about wood from him."

"I haven't the skill myself. These are all bought – or acquired. You'd be surprised what people are foolish enough to throw away."

Kathleen Dolan entered with a tray containing the tea set. Was it Royal Doulton? Bingham wasn't sure. He smiled to himself. Why was it that the rest of the world thought travellers were poor? He'd seen no signs of poverty: rough living on some of the sites no doubt, but trailers that must have cost an arm and a leg. He'd have liked to ask further, but good manners prevented him. Bingham knew he'd never have made a policeman.

"You live well, Mrs Dolan," he said, sipping his tea on one of the Chesterfields.

"We've seen all our girls properly married, Mr Bingham. We chose for them when they'd allow us, but they all had good fortunes come what may."

"Fortunes?"

Kathleen Dolan looked across at her husband. He nodded assent for her to continue. Pride was in the air, whether Bingham was of their kind or not.

"It's a tradition among our people that the bride's family pays what we call a 'fortune' to the husband when they marry."

Bingham waited, restrained by good manners or what his mother would have called 'breeding'; nevertheless, he was dying to know what a 'fortune' might mean. Paddy Dolan eased back into the unyielding leather of the sofa.

"At the turn of the century it would have been anything between £100,000 and £200,000. It was a matter of pride for a man to claim a good fortune. Amos O'Leary wanted more than his brothers had got."

"And you have the two daughters?"

"Three, but I've three sons to put up against it."

As a teacher, Bingham had never seen money of that kind, not even in his lump sum when he retired. He laughed at the contrary rewards of the world. Somewhere along the line, the man sitting opposite him had garnered a small fortune – sewn, nurtured and harvested.

Bingham knew the coupled waited to hear what he had to say about their granddaughter, but Bingham needed to choose his moment. He needed the atmosphere relaxed for what he had to do. Family was everything to these people, family and tradition; and both were breaking up around them. Even their home, the solid walls of the bungalow that must have set them back £250,000 couldn't protect them from the stormy changes ahead.

He sensed that Paddy Dolan was not an angry man, not one to rush at his problems fists flying, but he had a cross to bear and Bingham was the bringer of that cross. He'd known the truth or what he hoped might be the truth on that second day, as he'd talked with Martha in her trailer. Then, he'd no news to bring, but now it was different.

His policeman friend, ex-DCI Simon Brockie, had once told him that a detective only knew the criminal once he came to know the victim well. This he'd found to be true: it was usually the victim who provided the answers.

"I want you to come with me," he said, "I've someone I'd like you to meet. If Mrs Dolan came it would be good."

Bingham hadn't intended to involve Kathleen Dolan at this stage in his investigation, but this was before he'd met her. She was subservient to her husband – the men call the shots in the travelling community – but he felt that at the slightest hint of trouble hers would be the restraining voice.

Bingham had spent the previous night at home in Northfield, having caught the train from Colchester to Ipswich, where Lina had picked him up in their car. Ben was glad to see the farmhouse again, and Bingham had left the little terrier at home, preferring to tackle what he hoped was the final stage of his journey alone.

The car, a Hyundai i10 they'd bought only in March that year because Lina wanted a smaller vehicle, was parked outside the Dolan's bungalow. When Bingham opened the rear door for Kathleen Dolan to get in, Paddy, his tone more concerned than derisory, said:

"Are you expecting me to travel in that, Mr Bingham?"

"There's more leg room than you might think, Paddy."

"It's my bulk that concerns me. I'll not be able to move my elbows. Have you any objection if we go in the Jaguar?"

"None at all."

They travelled south on the A12 with Paddy Dolan at the wheel. When the Jaguar reached the outskirts of Colchester, Bingham directed the traveller to turn off onto the A134 and so along by the side of the Colne until they came to an hotel car park. Bingham felt the Dolans' anticipation rise.

"If you'll take a seat in the garden by the river, I'll be back in a jiffy," he said.

When he returned it was with a tray of drinks and a young woman. Like her mother, she was short but without the fat and dyed hair. In fact, her hair was a dark black and, like her father's, naturally wavy. Lizzie O'Leary had it trimmed and held close to her head by a bandana.

The joy on Kathleen's face was unrestrained, and on Paddy's held in check only by his masculine need to be in control and have an explanation; but they both hugged the girl and held her close for several minutes before allowing her to sit down.

Lizzie looked at Bingham as though needing his permission to speak, although he'd run through what she should say on the previous afternoon when he'd tracked her down following his visit to the Margaret and James Kinch. They sat, almost like a tableau, Paddy and Kathleen on one side of the picnic table, Lizzie and Bingham on the other, the river rippling by with the willow tree hanging over them in fresh leaf.

"I'm sorry Gran' Daddy and Gran' Mammy," she said, "I didn't mean to cause you sorrow but I seemed to have no choice."

The apology delivered, Lizzie looked at Bingham again, at a loss how to continue.

"Lizzie's working here at The New Inn," said Bingham, "as a trainee chef."

"You don't need a job, Lizzie," urged Paddy, "You're fine at home helping your Mammy ..."

It was Kathleen's touch on his arm that made the big man pause.

"Let the girl tell her tale, Paddy. She's the one we must listen to."

Bingham looked at Lizzie and smiled. She'd been frightened when he found her the previous afternoon but Bingham's natural stillness and quiet reassured the girl and she'd spilled out her story.

"Tell it to your granddad and grandma just as you told it to me."

"I had to get away. I didn't want to end up like me Mammy, stuck in the trailer looking after the kids all day ..."

"It's the man's job to provide for the family. There's nothing wrong with what your Mammy does."

"Oh, but there is, Gran' Daddy – look at her! I'm not saying me Mammy is a bad mother, but she's stuck in the trailer all day ..."

"There's plenty to do ..."

"Paddy," said Bingham, in the tone he'd used to bring unruly classes to order, "Lizzie's finding it difficult enough to explain, as it is. Your constant interruptions are going to make her clam up completely."

The anger in the old man's eyes was quietened once again by the touch of his wife's hand. Bingham nodded to Lizzie. The look she returned suggested she might run back into the hotel, but the young woman tried once more.

"You sound like Daddy, Gran' Daddy. He didn't want Mammy to do anything but stay at home and look after him and us kids. Cleaning and cooking and mending and seeing to the family's all very well but look at Mammy now. She's dead from the neck up through all the drudgery. Some days she doesn't want to get out of bed. I didn't want to end up like that. I had to get away ... It was a joke at first but Marti soon came to know I was serious ..."

"You didn't ..."

The hand stopped his question and Lizzie pressed on.

"I'm sorry about the stolen car. Have the people got it back? But it was the only way to get away. Marti got it going and we came down here. I knew there was family here. I was desperate. I didn't know what we were doing. We ... even went to ask the priest to marry us, we were so desperate. But he didn't and I was glad though I know you'll not be, Gran' Mammy ..."

Kathleen Dolan smiled but said nothing.

"It was Aunty Margaret who helped me. When I told her how I felt she asked me what I was going to do. I didn't know, and so she took me to the local college and the lady there asked me what I could do, and I said I could look after the kids and cook, and so she said did I want to train as a chef. I go to the college two days a week and I work here the rest of the time. I do lunch duty."

"Do you live with Margaret?" asked Kathleen.

"No. She got me a little room with a friend of hers. It's near here and so I can get to work easily. We start at six in the morning. I love it. I feel like a real woman now. It's nice having money in your pocket and not having to ask Daddy for it."

"Your Daddy will go mad when he knows what you've done, Lizzie, said Kathleen.

"He mustn't know. That's why I couldn't tell anyone – not until I was ready … It's nice here. I like turning up to work every day and seeing the tourists and guests arrive in their posh cars with their expensive clothes and luggage.

"It was difficult at first. The head chef didn't like me. She didn't think a traveller was to be trusted. She thought I was dirty. Country people think all travellers are dirty. But there's no one cleaner. Mammy always keeps our trailer spotless. You can see your face in the shiny surfaces and eat your dinner off the floor. That's what she always says. Even Daddy says that. So, I showed her, and when I'd cleaned the surfaces down just the once her attitude changed. She said she'd never seen anything like it."

Lizzie looked up at her grandparents who hadn't touched their drinks, so entranced were they by the girl's account, and smiled. She had them listening now, and continued:

"My main job is the chopping of the vegetables but I'm quicker than anyone they've ever seen and so I'm already helping with the cooking. When I pass my exams, I'll be promoted … I'm OK with the work but I need help with the reading …"

Lizzie blushed. She'd told Bingham that her reading skills were rudimentary, picked up in a scrappy fashion at the various schools where she'd spent only weeks before the family moved on.

"But reading the children's books to Tommy and Mary helped. It helped a little," she added, defensively.

"You'll not be able to hide away here forever, Lizzie," said Kathleen, "Sooner or later your Daddy's going to find out and come for you."

"Does Martin Boylan know where you are?" asked Paddy.

"Martin and me have done nothing wrong, Gran' Daddy."

"That's not what I'm saying. That's not what folks will be saying."

"He went straight back. The running away started as a joke but it turned out right for me. I can't go back."

"Your Gran' Daddy's right, Lizzie. You'll have brought shame on the family. You'll have a bad name for the rest of your life. You know it'll be hard finding a husband for you now, don't you – now you've been away with a man for the night?"

"Are you wanting to marry Martin Boylan?"

"I'm not wanting to marry anybody, Gran' Daddy. I'm not in love with Marti and he's not in love with me."

"He's got a lot to answer for ..."

"It's not his fault. Running away was my idea ... I know it was daft, but we were swept along with it. I wasn't thinking ..."

"You certainly weren't doing that!" snapped Paddy.

"I just wanted to get away. I keep saying that. I was desperate. What would have happened to me if I'd stayed at home? Do you remember Molly Callan?"

The question caused both Kathleen and Paddy to flinch. Their lips tightened, and Bingham detected both indignation and shame in their manner.

"Do you remember what happened to Molly?" Lizzie insisted.

There was no response. Lizzie went on.

"She was nice girl was Molly: lovely to look at – blonde hair and those lovely blue eyes. You couldn't but like Molly, but it made no difference did it? They cast her out."

Lizzie turned to Bingham.

"I was only a child then, but I could see it was wrong. She loved Tommy Caffrey, and they'd been going steady. That means they'd been out three or four times together and the families expected them to get married. That's the way it is with us. And Molly wanted to, but the women could all see that Tommy was no good. He came from a fighting family and was too handy with his fists. Even Molly's mother could see that any marriage wasn't going to be a good one, and I think that she might have stood up for Molly if Molly hadn't got herself pregnant. Traveller women of our kind are expected to be virgins on their wedding night.

"Before news got around, they were married, but it was a disaster from the start. Tommy Caffrey may have been a father but he was still a child and too fond of the women. He'd smarten himself up when he got in from work at night and go off drinking with his mates, leaving Molly at home. He didn't want her around, did he – not when he was out with his mates?

"When she protested, he knocked her around. Three kids down the line he was still knocking her around ...

You're looking troubled, Mr Bingham. Are you wondering why she didn't divorce him?"

Bingham wasn't – he'd already heard enough to know the answer to such a question – but Lizzie was in full flight and needed to say her piece. Bingham smiled and was silent.

"Divorce isn't an option among traveller people."

"Divorce is wrong," cut in Kathleen Dolan, "You know that Lizzie. Molly Callan made her bed. It was up to her to lie on it."

"It's not right. If I'd stayed on I might have ended up like Mammy or Molly Callan."

"You have to do things the traveller way, Lizzie, and that means you stay married for life whatever happens. We're Catholics, and a good Catholic isn't one for the divorcing. You exchange your vows before God and those vows are not for the breaking."

"But it's all right, is it, for the men to carry on with other women? Aren't they supposed to keep their marriage vows for life?"

Paddy and Kathleen looked at each other. There was guilt in their silence but not of a personal kind; it was more that they were aware of things they'd rather not acknowledge. Eventually, Paddy said:

"It's not your father you're talking about?"

"No, I don't know about Daddy. He likes the drink, but that's all I know. But the other men ..."

"Two wrongs don't make a right, Lizzie," said Kathleen, quietly, "It's the woman's place to hold the family together."

"If you leave the community, Lizzie, you'll be an outcast," said Paddy.

Bingham watched the young woman, knowing exactly what was going through her mind. Whatever friends she made among what she called the 'country people' (a nicer term, Bingham thought, than 'Gorgias' for anyone who wasn't a traveller), she would still be among strangers. If, later, she fell in love with one of these strangers then those she'd once called friends in the traveller community wouldn't speak to her.

"I'll not be treated like a whore, Gran' Daddy. I've done nothing wrong."

In the presence of such courage, Bingham decided to remain silent and let the tension take the day. It was clear that both Lizzie's grandparents were willing to forgive and forget, to pop the young woman in their Jaguar and return her safe and sound to her parents. More than anything else, this is what they wanted. She'd almost broken the rules of their culture but not quite, and there was still time to reclaim her.

"What would I do if I went back, Gran' Daddy – marry a traveller lad and have his children? Is that what I want for myself? Is that what you want for me?"

Bingham had done what he was asked to do: find a young woman who missing. It was the end of the search, the end of his fifth case, if he wanted to look at it in that way. As he watched the three Dolans, unable to answer the questions they'd raised, unable to find any kind of resolution that would bring about the happy ending they all craved, he thought back over his previous searches. Certainly, there had been resolutions of a kind, but resolutions that raised further questions and required further decisions before any road forward could be found for the protagonists; and they all warranted that word.

Chapter Nine

THE BRINGER OF BAD TIDINGS

As soon as he arrived home and had warded off the three dogs, Lina put her arms round Bingham's neck, kissed him and said:

"What's wrong, Bing?"

"Nothing."

"I can see it in your face."

"Lina, I'm shattered. There's no chance of my having a cat nap is there, while you wonder whether or not you have the ingredients for that penne dish you do – the one with the spicy, vegetarian sausage sauce?"

"There might be, provided I'm convinced you'll open up about what's troubling you while we eat it."

Twenty minutes was usually long enough for Bingham to shake off a torpor and he woke to a large glass of Barolo and the aroma of shallots, carrots, celery and sweet peppers cooking with rosemary and red onion sausages; coming from the kitchen, also, there was the smell of basil and Parmesan.

"I feel I ought to go and see Martha O'Leary. She was kind to me, and I'm not sure that she knows where Lizzie might be," said Bingham as he, quite literally, wolfed down the meal Lina had prepared.

"What's stopping you?"

"Fear."

"Amos?"

"Yes. I've no great desire to bump into him. Not very dignified, is it?"

"From what you told me at Paolo's, Mr O'Leary seems to be one to avoid. I can't say I blame you for that, Bing."

"No, you wouldn't, would you," Bingham replied with a smile and a squeeze of his wife's hand.

"Do you know where they went after Appleby?"

"Paddy seemed to think they'd be at Newark. Evidently, there's work there."

"Don't you think he'll go and see his daughter?"

"He wouldn't commit himself. He had to choose his side, and Lizzie is his prime concern."

"Sleep on it," replied Lina, know her husband had every intention of travelling to Newark the next day and wishing he hadn't.

The next day being Sunday, Bingham spent his time at home but on the Monday morning, leaving Michael Joyce and Ben behind but taking his flute with him, Bingham set off on the three-hour trip.

Paddy Dolan had been reluctant to give him any more information but since Newark had several travellers' sites, both council and private, he eventually agreed to Bingham's request for directions.

He wanted to find the travellers' site by midday at the latest and have a chat with Martha while, hopefully, Amos was seeking driveways to ruin. Slow traffic on the A14 didn't help and neither did a traffic jam on the A1 and so it was early afternoon before he reached the Newark area.

Leaving the A1 he found himself in shady lanes edged by low brick walls behind which were secreted houses and cottages, well-maintained, lovingly cared-for and apparently oblivious to the noise and bustle of the passing world. Paddy had told him that the site was a thirty-acre field bought by a member of the travelling community some years previously.

The sweet smell of summer assailed Bingham's nostrils: hedge-parsley and chervil, sweet-scented in leaf and blossom from the roadside banks, bracken and ash, briar roses and elder were in blossom, the branches of flowering limes overhung the road.

Lost in this splendid seasonal burst of energy, Bingham pulled up at one of the cottages where its owner, an elderly man, was hoeing his row of turnips.

"Excuse me," he said, "I'm looking for the traveller site."

"Are you from the council?" replied the man in a civil tone, looking Bingham up and down, "It's time they were moved on."

"A nuisance, are they?"

"It's not so much that as the fact they do as they like. They haven't got planning permission for the site but they're backwards and forwards with lorries full of bricks and tarmac all the time. I'm lucky if I can get permission to put up a conservatory on the back of my house."

"It doesn't seem fair ..."

"Fair! It's not exactly a level playing field is it? Why are these people outside the law? I'm not prejudiced against the people themselves. If we can live side by side in peace and harmony, then I've no complaints but the council seems frightened of them. Do you know how much they paid for that field at auction?"

"I've no idea."

"Twenty-eight thousand pounds! They're not exactly short of a bob or two, are they?"

"No," replied Bingham, who'd been surprised at how well-off the travellers he'd met seemed to be, "I take it they're not far along this road?"

"Round the next bend. Are you from the council?"

"No, I'm what you might call a 'friend of the family'."

He left the man gaping at him over the low, brick wall. Bingham didn't like prejudice but could see the justification for the man's grievance. Why did travellers seem to be outside the law? Were councils afraid of them? Why?

He came upon the site suddenly: an open field, bathed in sunshine, the family plots divided neatly by fence rails. Several horses padded around freely, tugging at the rich, fragrant grass. Bingham had always marvelled that such fully muscled, magnificent animals lived almost entirely on the simplest of vegetation.

He drove onto the site and parked his car for a quick getaway. One of the few men about who were erecting the fence rails approached him immediately.

"This is private property …"

"I know," said Bingham, cutting the man short, "I'm looking for Amos O'Leary and his family. Paddy Dolan tells me they're here and I've something for them."

"Amos is out at work."

"Martha will do just fine. It'll only take a few minutes and then I'll be on my way."

The man stood back and nodded towards what Bingham recognised as Marth's trailer. There were at least a dozen others on the site. Outside each, the women folk – none of whom Bingham recognised – were washing clothes in bowls overflowing with soap suds. Children were running free, playing tag, rolling on the warm ground, kicking balls about or playing with toys such as dolls and cars.

Once again, the scents of summer surrounded Bingham: brambles, foxgloves and pink campion in the hedges. Clouded-yellow butterflies hovered around the brambles and bees had their heads deep in the bells of the foxgloves.

At the far end of the site a few old trailers were the only eyesore. Bingham guessed they were cannibalised for their parts, dumped as they were in a higgledy-piggledy fashion at odds with those that were homes.

Martha saw Bingham before he saw her and stood rigid on the steps of her trailer as he approached. When he looked up, he was met with a gaze both hostile and contemptuous.

"You deceived us."

"I know, Martha."

"You weren't who you said you were."

"Has your father phoned you?"

"What's that to you?"

Bingham wasn't prepared to go through a long tit-for-tat conversation. He'd had enough of those while trying to find Lizzie. He pulled aside a chair that was tucked under Martha's washing bench and sat down.

"If Amos finds you here ..."

"I'm not really concerned whether Amos finds me or not. You people told me next to nothing; if I'd come as myself, you would have told me less than nothing. It was on the basis of two snippets of information that I found your daughter, but nevertheless I'd like to reassure myself that you know where she is and that she is not only safe but prospering. Now do we talk, or do I just get in my car and drive off. It's up to you Martha. You were kind to me, and I'd like to repay that kindness but I'm not playing 'oh yes you are, oh no you're not' all day."

Bingham knew it was the longest speech Martha had ever listened to outside a tittle-tattle gossip session with the other women, and he'd done it deliberately, both to intrigue her and to nettle her.

Martha said nothing but turned back into her trailer. When she emerged, five minutes or so later it was with a tray containing her Wedgewood tea set and a large cake. As soon as it appeared, her two children, Tommy and Mary, appeared from nowhere and hovered.

"You go away now," she said, handing each of them a large slice, "and leave Mr Joyce and me in peace."

"Have you brought your flute, Mr Joyce?" asked Mary.

"Would I dare come without it?"

"Off you go now," said Martha, a second time, "Mr Joyce and I haven't long."

Bingham sipped his tea slowly. It was strong, almost at odds with the dainty cup. Martha watched him and waited.

"Am I right in thinking you knew Lizzie was safe?"

"Katherine phoned and told me that much but wouldn't say more since she'd made Lizzie a promise. I was glad to know, but I'm still worried sick. I couldn't do more without Amos knowing, and that wouldn't have been … right."

"He'd have been after her?"

"In a flash. Lizzie's brought shame on herself and her family."

"She's a good girl, Martha. Running away – her idea, not Martin Boylan's – was more than a lark, although she didn't know that at the time. She's brought no shame on you."

"What's she doing, Mr Joyce?"

"Making a life for herself."

"Her life's here with the family."

"It's not the way the world's going, Martha."

Quietly and with all the gentleness he could muster, Bingham told Martha of Lizzie's plans. She listened with what in a woman less stoical, less accepting of the hard knocks life was expected to throw at you, would have been tears in her eyes. Twice she rose from her chair and walked off towards the end of her trailer; each time she returned, the look in her eyes had grown harder.

"How long will this be?"

"She'll start college proper in the autumn on the catering course, but by then Lizzie'll be well on with the practical side. She has her head screwed on, Martha, but she needs you. She needs to be able to come home and visit."

"Has my da agreed?"

"Paddy is like you, Martha – the old ways are best."

"She'll get caught up with a lad – I know our Lizzie – and then where will we be?"

Bingham knew what was in her mind, just as he knew mention of contraception was out of the question. He doubted whether the women even talked about it among themselves. Traveller women only slept with their husbands and a child conceived in that way could only be a blessing. He could see, also, that Martha saw her daughter moving into a house, turning her back on the travellers' way.

"There's no thought in her mind of settling down with what you call the country people, Martha. She wants ..."

How could he say that Lizzie didn't want to end up like her mother?

"She wants another way of life, Mr Joyce – I can see what you're driving at – but Lizzie can't have it both ways. Every time one of us moves into a house or settles down outside of being with us, our community is weakened further. She knows her father won't stand for it. She knows it'll break my heart."

"An education can only be a good thing, Martha ..."

"Can it? What good's it done the world? Are we any better for it, any more at peace with each other? The simple ways are best – the ways we all understand."

Listening to her mother, Bingham could easily understand why Lizzie, without even knowing exactly why, had simply run away. No arguments were going to persuade Martha that what Lizzie was doing was sensible, inevitable or acceptable.

He took his notebook from his pocket, wrote his phone number down and ripped out the sheet of paper.

"If you ever want to get in touch, Mar ..."

"Why should I want to do that? My daughter's gone. You'll not be telling me where she is, and if you did would she come back? No. You're the bringer of bad tidings, Mr Joyce or whatever your name is. You'd best be on your way."

Martha's voice had reached a shrill note, and Bingham knew he'd gain no further ground by talking. He placed the sheet from his notepad on the table, thanked Martha for the tea and cake and turned to go.

He was only a few hundred yards down the lane that led to the travellers' site, passing a small wood on his right that bordered the house of the man he'd spoken to on arrival and was accessed from the road through a five-barred gate, when he saw Amos O'Leary's truck approaching. Bingham pulled across into a passing place since the lane was narrow and waited for O'Leary to go by. The traveller held the centre of the lane, giving no ground at all, and turned to look down at the driver he'd obliged to pull over.

When he recognised Bingham, he slammed on the brakes, reversed and positioned his truck at an angle across the lane, impeding traffic both ways.

Bingham could have reversed an indefinite distance along the lane past the travellers' site, leaving O'Leary to pursue him, but pride and the thought that the traveller would run his new car into the bank prevented him. He stepped out of his car as O'Leary jumped down from his truck.

The traveller was shirtless, although the trousers he wore belonged to his salesman's suit and the braces that held them up clung to O'Leary's bare shoulders. The first punch to Bingham's solar plexus winded him and the second doubled him up in agony. Before he knew what was happening, O'Leary had grabbed him by the hair and dragged him through the gate and into the wood, where he threw Bingham to the ground and kicked him in the back.

"Up, get up! I'm going to teach you what it is to be a man and what it is to try and make a fool of Amos O'Leary."

The speech was accompanied by another kick: this time to the back of Bingham's thighs. He struggled to his knees, and O'Leary's right foot caught him in the stomach causing him to double up again and collapse onto the leaves and twigs of the forest floor.

"I shan't be telling you again – up!"

Rarely had been Bingham been involved in a fight. Once, he'd knocked a man who was hitting his girlfriend to the ground, but this had been unusual: right had been on Bingham's side and the man had not retaliated. Usually, however, he'd talked his way out of trouble or given the impression by his manner that hitting him wouldn't be a good idea. None of these strategies was going to work with O'Leary.

Bingham knew that if he stood, he'd be knocked down again, and if he remained where he was, he'd be kicked mercilessly. He also knew he'd stand no chance in any kind of fight against O'Leary: a man younger and stronger than him, a man bruised by many a bare-knuckle fight.

"Up!"

Bingham struggled to his feet. Before he'd straightened himself, O'Leary's fist smashed into his left cheek. Bingham felt a tooth or a crown loosen and shift itself in his mouth. Ridiculously, he felt the need to retrieve the loosened piece if it was a crown. While this thought was passing through his mind, O'Leary's other fist caught Bingham under the jaw, and he fell heavily backwards, lessening the impact of his fall by reaching behind him with both hands. O'Leary's right foot, still immaculately shod in his patent leather salesman's shoes, rested itself on Bingham's abdomen and pushed him to the ground.

"You're hardly worth the fighting, but I'll know from you where my daughter is, or I'll leave you good as dead in the wood."

Bingham's lips were swelling rapidly and the pain in his left cheek made him wonder whether his jaw was broken. He could barely speak, but in the scramble of his thoughts he wondered how much O'Leary knew and who had told him.

"Martha's father phoned, and I got it from her," he replied in answer to Bingham's question.

"Martha doesn't know ..."

"I know that – Martha wouldn't lie to me – but you do, and I'll have it from you."

"Amos ..."

"Don't 'Amos' me. Whoever you may be, you're a dossa as far as I'm concerned – a dossa who lied and cheated his way into the bosom of my family, and I'll have answers from you."

"We need to sit ..."

O'Leary's fist took Bingham fully in the mouth. Bingham stumbled but didn't fall, and so O'Leary kicked his feet from under him. The travellers' own right foot thudded down intended for Bingham's knee, which it would have dislocated had he not rolled himself into a ball by tucking his knees up into his chin.

Knowing he made a pathetic sight crouched on the ground, Bingham struggled to his feet once more.

"Lizzie needs ..."

Again, a barrage of punches took Bingham's breath away. Blood ran from his forehead and trickled from his mouth. He took his breathes in short gasps between the punches, panting like a woman in labour. He thought of Lina, as he did his best to fend off the blows and the pain.

How much more he could take Bingham was unsure, and the thought was met by the uncertainty of how he could finish the brawl; that there would be no cavalry riding to his rescue he knew. In the end, after O'Leary had expended his frustrations further, it was a woman's voice that saved Bingham; he heard Martha call out to her husband.

"Haven't you done enough, Amos? Do you want his death on your hands?"

O'Leary looked up and leaned forward, poised for another round of punches, his fists circling up and down in agitation.

"Stay out of this, Martha. This is man's work. I'll know where my daughter is."

"I know where she is," said Martha.

"You what?"

"You heard."

O'Leary blinked away the sweat running from his brow. He, too, was puffing with the effort of his punches. Shoving Bingham aside, he turned to his wife.

"Are you telling me ...?"

"I'm telling you. Now lay off him ... He's not worth it."

Bingham watched the couple eyeing each other and wondered what the hell he was going to do if O'Leary attacked his wife. The traveller was leaning against a tree, his right arm supporting his weight, his left swinging loosely. Martha stood by the open gate, her arms hanging by her side and her feet slightly apart. What had brought her to the wood, Bingham had no idea. Was it the noise of his beating, the sound of snapping twigs and leaves or had she seen the truck angled across the road?

If O'Leary went for his wife, Bingham would have to do something if it was only to leap on his back or shove his head hard against the tree in the hope of knocking him out.

The woman's eyes never left her husband's. He was master in the house and his word was law; in challenging him, Martha had gone against traveller tradition. A wife didn't defy her husband; what he wanted he got, and Martha wasn't about to throw aside custom for the likes of a dossa, was she?

'He's not a bad man – O'Leary … Daddy said I brought out the best in him, and he loves me – I know that to be true.' Martha's words came back to Bingham as he watched and wondered.

The stand-off seemed to last ages. In the end it was the woman who took the field. Amos turned and looked at Bingham, his anger apparently replete. Martha took her husband's arm and the couple made their way to the truck without looking back, leaving Bingham to wonder what he'd achieved that day.

Chapter Ten

AN INCONVENIENT SHADOW

"I'm sorry for the beating you took, Mr Bingham," said Lizzie O'Leary.

She'd made the same remark a dozen or more times since the summer on almost every occasion Bingham had come to Colchester to teach her to read, but Bingham listened yet again because it was something the young woman had to say, something she had to expunge from her soul.

Autumn was creeping in after a dry summer, the river was low and the willow tree already dropping leaves; but Lizzie's mood was ebullient. Everybody had kept their word. Paddy and Kathleen, hoping their granddaughter would "see sense and return to the traveller way", had said nothing to her father, and Martha had somehow contrived to keep Amos in the dark. Lizzie's college course had begun, the summer had put money in her pocket and her circle of friends had widened.

Lina had come down with her husband when the lessons dropped to one a week and her womanly presence encouraged the girl to speak.

"I've not made much of me being a traveller," she'd said on one such occasion, "not because I'm ashamed of my culture but because people who don't know me are prejudiced. The people I work with are fine now, but it wasn't always so."

"Society will change," replied Lina, not for the first time, "but it takes a while. Besides, it isn't just us – the country people – who need to change."

"No, I know that's true. If only Mammy could trust Daddy to be more reasonable, I know she'd visit me."

"Has she not been down at all?" asked Lina.

"I've not seen her since I left in May."

"It's only a few months, Lizzie. Your Mum's had to take a lot in. It's all been too much, too soon. She'll come around."

Their conversations always drifted around the same subjects. The weight of her conscience was heavy on Lizzie O'Leary, but she remained optimistic and her mood was never low for long.

On this occasion, she'd asked Bingham and Lina to visit her, and both felt it marked a parting of the ways, a moving on. They sat at the table where Bingham had first brought her grandparents to meet the young woman and Lizzie insisted on paying for the meal. While they were waiting to order, she said:

"There's someone I'd like you to meet."

A young man appeared, almost out of nowhere as Lizzie had done. He came over, looking sheepish and holding out his hand in a gesture of welcome.

"I met Barry when he came here for a meal with friends. I was waiting at table that day because we were so busy. He asked me for my phone number, but I wouldn't give it to him at first, would I?"

Barry smiled and blushed.

"He isn't a traveller, but he knows I am, and you don't mind, do you?"

Barry shrugged as though the matter was of no importance.

"We've been out together now a lot of times, haven't we? And I feel free in a way I never could with a traveller man. Traveller women are expected to behave in a certain way. It's like playing a role."

Bingham, never one to indulge in an outflow of emotion with strangers, sympathised with the young man's embarrassment; but there was no denying Lizzie's honesty or her need to share their relationship with someone. Bingham looked at his wife and saw the encouragement she was offering the younger woman simply by the expression in her eyes.

"We've never done anything my culture would consider wrong. Barry respects me. It was a month before we kissed, wasn't it? I've never been happier."

"How about another round of drinks before the meal comes?" said Bingham, "Would you give me a hand, Barry?"

Relieved, the young man accompanied Bingham to the bar and held him in conversation even after the drinks arrived.

"You realise what you're taking on, do you, son?"

"I think so."

"She's a lovely girl is Lizzie, and a brave one – a pioneer, really – but she's up against it, and will need all the strength you've got to support her."

"I can manage that, I think."

"I'm sure you can, Barry, I'm sure you can."

Had Lina drawn the young man aside, she'd have asked if he loved her, but Bingham couldn't go down that road.

"I take it she's told you about her family?"

"Yes. Her mum seems OK, and her grandparents. It's the father who might be a problem."

"Amos is all right, but he has a temper on him."

"Lizzie says he's never hit her or any of her brothers and sisters or their mum."

"I'm sure that's true, but it doesn't mean he wouldn't have a go at you. Just take things steady."

"Yeah – we will."

"You need to appreciate why Lizzie's community will be unhappy about her taking up with someone who isn't a traveller. Each time that happens is another blow to a whole way of life. Their culture is under fire. One day it may disintegrate completely, and Lizzie is in the vanguard of that destruction."

"We'll respect her ways."

"Yes, I'm sure you will."

"It was bound to happen, Bing," said Lina as they drove home, "She's a young woman and a passionate one, and young women don't half fancy young men. He's very good looking."

"Did she say that?"

"Say what?"

"Don't half fancy?"

Lina laughed and leaned back in the passenger seat.

"What else did she say?"

"That she'd already had a spot of bother with some traveller women who she bumped into in Colchester one day."

"Bother?"

"She was with Barry and they spat at her. She's a brave girl. Her real problems will come with family weddings and funerals. Can you imagine being an outcast at such events?"

It wasn't really a question, and Bingham offered no opinion. They sat in silence for some time, the Suffolk countryside passing them by as they left Ipswich along the Valley Road and drove the last few miles to their home in Northfield. The horse chestnut trees were already beginning to shed their leaves. A flock of starlings passed overhead looking for the berries of late summer: young and hungry.

"I just wish she'd taken things one step at a time."

"It's called love, Bing. Barry is a ray of sunshine in her life, not a shadow."

"I know, I know, and I'm sure you're right. You always are, where matters of the heart are concerned. It's just inconvenient at the moment, that's all."

Spring and Late Summer 2017

ACKNOWLEDGEMENTS

Although this story is a fiction, its key events are based on actual incidents and the experiences of people involved in similar situations and circumstances. Anyone wishing to delve deeper into the real world from which this novel is drawn should read:

Gypsy Girl by Rosie McKinley
Hodder and Stoughton 2011
Gypsy Boy by Mikey Walsh
Hodder and Stoughton 2009

All the characters in the book are fictitious, and any resemblance to persons living or dead, is purely coincidental.